CW00864779

John James

To Louise

Have a Merry Xmas
and try not to have
nightmares Mwahahahaha!!
Love John
x

This book is dedicated to the dark side

that dwells within us all

Also by the author

Unnatural Selection

The Rose

SICK vol 2 (released 2017)

Pandora's Kiss (released 2017)

Stories within

“Every evil is a sickness of soul…”

Saint Basil

Love Kills

Love Kills

I sat at corner table in Starbucks on Russell Street in Covent Garden. London was the home of 260 outlets in Greater London, but this one I liked more than any other being close to the square where street performers juggled, clowned and performed magic. The fact that it was unbelievably busy was the very reason I'd travelled from my apartment in Nothing Hill to be here. Here one was alone, anonymous, invisible. Here one could sit for hours watching people enter and leave, make up lives for them, imagining what they do for a living, what their home was like, what their partner was like, who they were banging on the side, what their flesh tasted like, how much they would bleed if you used a thin bladed knife to cut them open.

Three men stand by the counter waiting for seats to become free. All three are dressed in suits, expensive though probably not a name; two wore ties one plain one polka dot, both polyester... They probably spent all their money on the suits trying to look successful, poor bastards. As they chatted they scoped the room, three pairs of eyes scanning like lasers and, like a military targeting system settle on two women who seem young enough to be their daughters.

The two women, girls really, are sat at a table in the middle of the room. They are both in their early 20s, both with blonde hair, both in halter tops and tight black jeans, but only one could carry the look off. She had a firm looking body, her abdomen snare drum tight with a navel piercing with a purple stone, this surrounded by a tattoo of what look like doves, but from this distance I can't really tell. She has another tattoo on her left arm, this I can see and it's of a heart with a lightning bolt cutting through it, it's ugly and crass and makes her look cheap. She plays with her hair as she talks, winding it around her finger before letting it fall and repeating. I find it erotic and annoying at the same time and find myself wondering what she looks like naked, then, as an afterthought, what she looks like naked but with her arms cut off to rid her of that God awful tattoo.

Her friend is attractive too but less so. Her tits are bigger which is nice but her abs are not tight, not even toned, I'm not saying she's fat, but between where her top ends and her jeans begin the flesh is... Well... Squidgy. She giggles, a lot, probably thinking how much she wants to slash her friends face for being hotter.

An older couple sit on the far side of the room, him in a white shirt and plaid slacks with braces, his shoes are brown and scuffed, his face is pale and lined, his hair salt and pepper, mostly salt. She's wearing a flower print dress with a fake Pearl necklace and black flat heeled slip on shoes. Her face is lined too but it glistens in the evening sunlight, moisturized to within an inch of its life. Her hair is dark brown which looks fake, grey hairs at her temples stand as identifying markers to a bad dye job.

They sit in silence facing each other but staring past each other, after years of being together, having literally nothing to say. I can't discern their age, but I'd say sixties and wonder if they have children and when they stopped having sex, and do they even love each other anymore or are they just each other's habit now after all this time.

Those questions bring to mind why I am here in the first place. I'm here to hide away, to become invisible to possibly become a piece of entertainment for someone like me, an observer. I wonder what they'll make up about me. Nothing near the truth I'm sure of that.

I'm here, not only to disappear, but also to escape. I'm married you see, well, not married but I may as well be. I'm seeing someone, a girl, beautiful yes, but only on the outside and even that is not what it used to be. She's emotional, anger being the dominating emotion, angry about everything, the things I say, the things I do, the things I don't do. My girlfriend, Maria, hair long and dark mahogany, eyes deep brown so dark as to be almost black, a face so smooth and delicate and yet can twist and harden and scowl, a rabid dog of a face when things aren't perfect which, to be honest, is most of the time. Her frame is small and slim with athletic legs and arms, a tight arse and flat stomach sans belly ring and tattoo and great tits. But all this is ruined by an attitude that is similar to that that killed Jews in WWII.

This morning it started again, just the odd word slipping out like a child with Tourette's "bastard", "wanker". There was no explanation for these singular expletives ejected in my direction. I'm sure that Maria's psychopathy held some symbolic meaning for her, some imagined slight or wrong doing on my part.

As the morning moved on these pin pricks became verbal knife slashes, insults thrown at me like rocks, hurting, injuring my heart, my very soul. I don't know what aggrieved her, she never really makes that clear, just a collection of Lilliputian mistakes that make up the giant that looms over me fuelled to life by her anger. Maria is aggressive, physically as well as verbally, throwing punches like she's in some Rocky movie, she's strong, and coupled with the insults, the remarks that I'm ugly or old or insignificant, the injuries mount.

I could walk away, but like a pup beaten by its owner I stand scared, diminutive and an overwhelming feeling of loneliness. Maria seems unaffected by the carnage she is causing. She speaks as if speaking to a beetle, small and insignificant, irritating and ripe for stepping on, which she does metaphorically. I am sport for her, a way to make her feel powerful, in control. My weakness fuels her rage, my inability, or just plain reluctance, to fight back increasing her anger exponentially.

Eventually I leave, unable to take it anymore. I travel across London until I find myself here in Starbucks my mind black and violent, my teeth grinding, my brow furrowed. I want to go back tell her that I'm sorry, although I don't know what for. I want things to be good, to be normal, but I know that this is just a fantasy I have, things can never be normal, not with Maria.

I sip my coffee and watch the evening slash the throat of day and blackness pour from the wound. My phone sits in front of me silent and still, she hasn't called all day.

Boredom, or that's what I use as an excuse, drives me from the coffee shop and I head back to my apartment in Notting Hill. The evening is cold, my breath plumes from my mouth taking on a physicality and swirling about my face. People pass me, their heads half shrunken into their coats hurrying to their homes, bars, cafes, wherever. A homeless man sits on the corner, tin can at his feet, sign on his lap that reads *I'm blind and hungry, please help me.* I kick the can as I walk past, change scatters like leaves in the Autumn across the pavement. He calls after me, calling me names, his sightless head unable to locate me.

I arrive home just before eight and the light is gone from the sky, just an inky blackness. She's there waiting. I enter the apartment, a smile, though crooked, is set in my face. She does not return my smile.

"You need to get out of my life, " she says immediately without preamble, her eyes burning into me. "I hate you."

"I love you," I say, my heart now racing, Heart Attack City.

She scoffs, a deriding laugh at my statement of love. "You don't love me," she growls. "What have you ever done for me?"

I don't answer as no answer is the right one, I have learned this much.

"I don't love you," she is saying. "I don't know if I've ever loved you. You're not exactly a catch are you?"

I stand still like a statue unable to move, my heart throwing itself against my rib cage, my breath caught in my throat, I'm unable to speak.

She continues. A rampage. She takes me apart, dissects me with her words removing flesh, breaking bone, scooping out my organs, stamping on my heart. She tells me I'm scum, a piece of shit. She tells me she's embarrassed to be seen with me, that her friends warned her not to go with me, that I'm too old, too unattractive, too... I don't know, I can't take it in. I can feel my mind shatter, shards of my own cognition shredding the inside of my brain like hot shrapnel. I move towards the cabinet. It stands in the corner of the living room, a charity shop buy that I paid very little for but was, and still is, very sturdy and polished. I open the second drawer down, the echoes of insults ringing in my ears.

I take out a hammer that I had bought just two days previously. I feel the weight in my hand, close my eyes, concentrate on how it feels.

I hear Maria approach from behind, the growls of rage carrying words I know will hurt me, but I'm not listening now. At once I turn, blindingly I swing the hammer not knowing even if she is close enough to be in danger, but the sound, solid and satisfying, tells me she is. For a second there is silence save the sound of her body hitting the floor. She is stunned, blood runs from the side of her head. She looks up at me, opens her mouth to scream at me but the second hammer blow stops this.

I stand over her feeling in control for the first time since we met, but still a little scared. She is confused, knocked senseless by the hammer. When she tries to sit up I hit her again, not hard this time, just hard enough to drop her to the floor again, making sure she stays down. While she is lying there unable to move for an instant I sit astride her pinning her to the floor with my weight. I smile down at her without humour or affection. She seems helpless now, tiny and helpless.

"You fucking bitch," I hiss then lean in and say, "you fucking cunt."

She hates that word and it felt good to say it. I see her shake her head trying to regain some clarity, but before she can come around fully I spring into action. I climb off her and run into the kitchen. I pull drawers open taking out what I need, lighter fluid, a large knife, a steak knife and superglue. With my kit in hand I return to Maria who is holding her head and attempting to stand.

"Who told you to move, bitch," I say before striking her again with the hammer sending her down a third time.

I sit astride her again. I lift each hand and squeeze superglue on to the backs of both hands, push them to the floor and place my knees in her palms and pin her for a few seconds letting the superglue do its job. When I release her her hands are stuck firm to the floor. I slap her hard just for fun and then again and again, her face swelling under her eyes. Now Maria begins to scream for the first time, realizing, a little late, the predicament she is in. I enjoy the screams for a few seconds before I stop it, or at least change it to a frightened growl, by pouring lighter fuel in her eyes, spilling it into her mouth. I stab her breasts with the steak knife just for fun as she chokes on the lighter fluid, spitting it out, desperate to breathe. I sit there, bloody knife in hand, thinking of all the times she had insulted me, called me names, belittled me. With those thoughts, my one true clarity I force her mouth open wide, she fights this, but she is weak. I reach into her open mouth and, gripping her tongue tight in my fingers, I pull it out of her mouth and, with the large bladed knife, I slice it off. As Maria begins to choke on her own blood I hold the severed tongue to my ear and say, "What baby? What did you say?"

I toss the tongue to one side and stab her neck with the steak knife without even thinking. I cut her face to remove her of her beauty and douse her in the face again with lighter fluid.

She's struggling now, trying to pull her superglued hands from the floor and kicking out with her feet. She is also trying to scream, but with so much blood in her throat from her cut out tongue they are wet guttural sounds rather than screams. Her body jerks in full panic mode so much so that I have to climb off her. I stab her a few times in the breasts, stomach and legs and spray the wounds with lighter fluid. She passes out from the pain a couple of times but I rouse her with a slap.

I'm hard now, aroused at seeing the woman I love suffering as I have done and I masturbate above her face, it takes no time at all excited as I am. I come in her tongueless mouth. I'm spent now and it felt good, better than any sex I'd ever had with Maria, and that was good sex.

I lean over her, still excited, and bite her face, sometimes coming away with pieces of flesh between my teeth, a slice of cheek, a fragment of a lip. She's sobbing now, trying to scream in fear and pain, but her body is too weak to fight anymore and it jerks, seizure like, her body partly shutting down but fighting to survive at the same time.

I start to get bored so I get myself hard again and pull off her panties now soaked with urine and dirtied with faeces. I fuck her just for old times' sake, the warmth of her blood on my chest, her hot frightened breath in my ear. I scream out excitedly when I come. I whisper, "I love you," and lie on top of her for a minute or two listening to her cry.

Eventually, I get up and look down at my pathetic girlfriend. I spit on her before, out of desperation of what to do next, I take the large bladed knife and cut off her head. It takes time, but it's worth it. I hold up Maria's severed head and look at it, the beauty eliminated by my own hand, destroyed with knife and teeth. I look into the eyes and smile. I can see her teeth through the holes I've bitten in her cheek and she looks like she's snarling. But her eyes are my favourite feature, gone is the look of hatred and disgust replaced now by unadulterated fear.

I draw the head near. "I love you," I say. I kiss what remains of her lips. "I love you."

Little Darlings

Little Darlings

Part One

I sat in the classroom feet up on my desk trying to look suitably interested in a drab eight-year-old boy giving a monotone rendition of some poem by Wilfred "boring as fuck" Owen. The rest of the kids were bored, some checking facebook on their phones beneath their desks thinking I couldn't see them; some heavy eyed, tried desperately to look as if they were at least present. One girl, Amanda Ricliffe, sat staring at me, her deep blue eyes never moving from my face. I wanted to stare back, bore my eyes into hers or look at her pasty legs that stuck out from beneath her desk, make her feel uncomfortable, or better still, scared, but something stopped me.

A knock on the door took my eyes to my left where the freckle laden face of Miss Highgrave stared at me through the small glass windows in the classroom door. She beckoned to me and, despite my wanting to get back to frightening eight-year-old Amanda, I stopped the class.

"Kevin, I'm sorry I have to stop your fascinating poetry reading, but I'm needed. All of you discuss what the poem meant please."

I got slowly up from my seat and joined Miss Highgrave in the corridor. The English teacher was in her early twenties, not too pretty but her body made up for that. She wore a low cut sleeveless summer dress that plunged to reveal the smooth silky skin of a large bosom that dipped sharply into the tiniest waist. I knew of three male members of staff who had already tried to bed her, and one female member of staff, but all had been rebuffed.

"I have some bad news," she said without preamble.

I drew my eyes from her cleavage, my attention caught. I said nothing just tilted my head to one side, my body language asking the question.

“It's about Marilyn Fitzpatrick," she said, sadness brushing the edge of her words. "She was found this morning."

"Thank god," I breathed, "I've been worried about her."

Miss Highgrave stood stock still, her bottom lip quivering, her hands squeezing into tight fists and relaxing repeatedly. "She's been found dead," she said, "like the others." Pause. "She was..." pause. "Raped." With this her body exploded with emotion, her breasts began to rise and fall rapidly, tears burst from the corners of her eyes and she began to make strange sounds of grief like that of an asthmatic seal.

I tried to twist my face into a look of horror but covered my face with my hands when I felt a smile emerge. Little Marilyn was the fourth child to be murdered in the last six months. Two girls and one boy had already died at the hands of a monster. Their innocence had been taken, two tiny virginas ripped apart and the boy’s sphincter destroyed by the sexual act all ante-mortem. And the killer had not stopped there, while the children screamed and panicked they had been worked on with a razor blade, cuts covered their tiny bodies, cigarette burns peppered their soft flesh. The two girls had had several of their fingers and toes literally pulled off with pliers, deep bite marks on their inner thighs and their face. The boy's body had been defecated on as well as having his jaw broken so badly it sat on his tiny chest.

"Are you in shock," Miss Highgrave was saying.

I realised that I had been quiet for a long time and that my smile had grown while in my revelry. I pulled my features into something that resembled distress, raised my head to look at her and hoped she bought it.

"I think you should cancel you class and go home," she said, her voice still shaking with emotion. "All the children did come from your class."

I nodded slowly. "I guess you're right," I said back, trying to force out a tear, which I surprised myself by doing. "Thank you for telling me."

I ended the class that day without explanation much to the joy of the students. I left the room and the building feeling more and more joyful with every step, but as I reached the car park my heart sank. A man stood leaning against my car. He was tall with broad shoulders that suggested he worked out. His suit was a nice fit but cheap looking, guess he couldn't afford an Armani on a cop’s salary. His face had a strong jaw and hard stone grey eyes that stood in contrast to his jet black hair that was slicked back like he was some *Goodfellas* extra. He stood up straight and smiled as I approached, I did not return his grin.

The man held out his hand. "Detective Mason," he said as if I was supposed to be impressed.

"And?" I said ignoring his greeting.

"I've come about the murdered child," he said. "Marilyn Fitzpatrick." Unnecessary clarification added.

“And?" I said again.

"Can we..." pause, "chat?"

"Why?" I said immediately.

The cop rubbed his face with both hands and released a short sigh. "I'd rather do this at the station," he said, tinged with frustration? "Car parks ain't really my thing, for interviews in any case."

My eyebrow raised inquisitively. "That changed quickly from a chat to an interview," I said. "Am I under investigation, detective?"

The bastard laughed, a short snort of a laugh filled with derision. "Not unless you've done anything worth investigating,” he said through his laugh.

I thought about telling him to go fuck himself but must admit I wanted to hear this, I also wanted to hear what he had to say about Marilyn's injuries.

“Let's talk," I said eventually. "We'll take your car."

As the detective led the way to his shitty Honda on the other side of the car park I saw Amanda Ricliffe out of the corner of my eye. I turned to face her and she looked directly at me, but her eyes did not judge me or question, they caressed me, her lips parting slightly and her small tongue played along their edges.

"Something wrong?" Detective Mason asked.

I pulled my eyes from Amanda and turned back to the cop. "Let's get this over with," I said and got into the passenger seat of the car.

The questions I was asked were built upon one indisputable fact...the victim and the three previous victims had one common denominator, they all attended my class. I was asked simple questions like what did I teach and what was Marilyn like to teach. These questions, even in their simplicity had their purpose; one: to make me feel comfortable in their familiarity and two: to illicit a truthful response so that the men listening in from behind the two way mirror could develop a baseline for the purpose of comparison with my vocalisations when the real questioning began.

When they did come it was like I was in a movie, those corny detective dramas – *"Where were you on the night of...?"* and *"How well did you know the victim?"* I answered them all calm and with a clarity so as to not have my words misinterpreted. I could see Detective Mason slowly become agitated by my overall steady demeanour and even tone of voice. The only time I hesitated and lost composure internally was when I was confronted with the crime scene photos. Detective Mason opened a manila envelope and slid eight by six glossy colour photographs across the table and set them in front of me one by one. Each photo showed the true face of horror. I had known Marilyn Fitzpatrick, but these photos of her were unrecognisable as the eight-year-old blonde girl I'd known. Her tiny body was laid twisted unnaturally in what looked like an alley by the surrounding garbage. She was naked, her hands bound behind her back, her head tossed back, mouth open in a scream, her left eye half way down her cheek still attached to the socket by slim black looking nerves. There were cuts all over her and in places the skin had been flayed off completely.

I could feel my cock getting hard all of a sudden, the arousal I felt looking at this destroyed little girl was making it hard to control my emotions. I imagined the pain she must have endured, her small frame going into shock. I knew that most of these injuries had been inflicted ante-mortem and I knew without being told that she had been raped.

I pushed the photos to one side though my mind urged me to keep looking. "Why did you show me these horrible photos?" I said, my sincerity sounding more genuine to my ear than expected.

Detective Mason looked at me as if examining my physiognomy for fraudulent signs. "I wanted you to see what a mess was made of this innocent child," he said.

"Well, you're sick," I spat flexing my acting skills. "You do know I lost a child of my own last year don't you?"

"I do," he nodded.

"Then you are even sicker than I could ever imagine," I said. "You put these photographs in front of me knowing that inside I would die a little. I have every mind to sue for causing me such pain."

I looked the detective in the face and through the stone I saw hairline cracks, a slight hint that he felt he was losing this one. As quickly as I'd seen those signs of weakness he regained composure.

"I am sorry for your loss, I truly am," he said with no sincerity. "I see these bodies and I can't help but want to get the bastard who did this, you understand?" He didn't wait for me to respond. "The one factor that connects all four victims..."

"Is that I taught all four," I said cutting him off.

"Exactly," he said throwing a finger in my direction. "So you see why you're here. This," he stabbed the photographs with a solid finger, "does not in any way show the true picture, this shows a fraction of what this little girl went through."

"What do you mean?" I couldn't help it, I involuntarily leaned forward and my voice sounded excited in my head. I tried to calm.

"You guessed the child was raped, right?"

I nodded.

"Well," he said sitting back and knitting his fingers across his solid abs. "Well, she also had some of her teeth pulled out and she was found with toothpicks pushed deep into her rectum, all ante-mortem. The eye being gouged out," he pushed the related photo towards me. "Our ME thinks that this was the final straw for little Princess and she died of shock."

I was breathing heavy now my excitement at fever pitch. I could feel a fist of tension in my chest and my throat was dry like a desert in the height of summer. "I don't need to hear this," I lied. "It's just too upsetting."

Detective Mason leaned across the table, he strong jaw jutting out. "You need to hear this, Victor," he said becoming familiar. "These are the facts, an educated man like you must appreciate facts."

"You're not charging me with anything, I want to leave," I demanded.

I saw the detective look in the direction of the two way mirror and...was that a shrug? Was that defeat I saw on his face?

A few moments later the door opened and a brunette WPC walked into the room. She ignored the detective and spoke directly to me. "You can go now, sir. Thank you for your assistance."

I got up from my seat and turned to Detective Mason. "Goodbye," I said with a grin.

The WPC looked in the direction of the detective and then at me with a strange quizzical look, she could obviously feel the tension in the room.

I left the interview room and walked towards the exit, every pair of eyes judging me accusingly. As I hit the street I felt the chill of the air and pulled up the collar of my jacket and looked around for a taxi. I needed to get home to my wife before she got worried. As I made my way to the taxi rank I saw a young girl standing across the road staring me. I glanced at her and saw that it was Amanda Ricliffe. I tried to ignore her but her stare was magnetic and I had to look at her. A smile played on her lips and her hand seemed to be rubbing the front of her dress. I wanted to think that I was imagining her behaviour, that it was a misinterpretation of innocence on my part, but there was something about her actions that was mature far beyond her eight short years.

A taxi pulled up beside me putting itself between myself and Amanda.

"Want a taxi?" the driver said in a thick Asian accent.

I looked at the man and nodded. I opened the door and climbed into the back seat. I looked out of the windows across to where Amanda Ricliffe had been standing, but she was gone. I sat back in my seat, sweat soaking my back, my head suddenly hurting. I closed my eyes and instantly I saw blood, gallons of blood, and in that sea of red were the torn, mutilated bodies of children, naked with eyes and limbs missing, with their genitals destroyed, some with holes in their chests where their heart had been cut out.

"Where to, mister?" the taxi driver was asking irritably.

"Sorry," I said. I gave him the address and relaxed into my seat. I closed my eyes again trying to recapture the images I'd had just a few seconds ago, but they were different now, black and white and muted like a distant dream. Instead I thought of my wife and my mother waiting for me. Would they be worried or angry at my lateness? I hated an atmosphere at home and prayed that they would know about little Marilyn Fitzpatrick and be sympathetic.

The drive home gave me time to relax disturbed only by brief images of Amanda Ricliffe, like her photo was spliced into my transient thoughts. What was wrong with that girl? Why did she behave like she did? I wondered what her parents must be like for her to be so sexual so young. She wanted me I could tell, but it was wrong on so many levels. I shook my head to clear my mind of her and when that didn't work I pinched myself hard on my inner thigh until my eyes watered.

I refocused my mind on the interview I'd just attended going over every detail to see if I had slipped up in any way, had I dug myself a hole that could get me deeper into trouble? I decided I had not, but I'd only been at the school, in the town even, for just over a year and already there were problems. I did not want problems, I needed peace.

The taxi dropped me off outside my house and drove away at speed cursing me when I did not tip him. I stood for a moment looking up at my detached four bedroom home with its large back garden and wine cellar, a little upmarket for the area. I took a deep breath and walked up my driveway and let myself in. “Hello,” I called. No answer. I worked my way through the house looking for life. It seemed dark though the curtains were open and the sun shone bright outside, it was as if light did not want to enter. Instead I stood by the kitchen sink and looked out over the back garden, the green carpet interrupted now and then by patches of deep brown soil ready for planting. My mother was the gardener in the family, her friend Jacob would dig over the garden to her specifications and then she would plant vegetables or flowers. I was glad that she had a hobby to keep her busy, but I didn’t like Jacob, he was strong and sinewy with a waxed chest and designer stubble and he would talk inappropriately about my mother.

“Your mother is a beautiful woman,” he would say. “I want to taste her peach, feel her mouth on my skin.”

I would tell him to stop, demand that he never speaks of her again, I even told him never to come to my home again, but he'd never listen, threatening to turn my mother against me if I tried to shut him out of our lives.

"I want to take you mama from behind," he'd say. "Fuck her while you watch, fuck her pussy, her ass..."

"Victor?"

The mention of my name shocked me out of my thoughts, and I was grateful for it. I turned to see my mother. She was slim and attractive with white hair and shocking blue eyes. She wore a long flowing dress of pale brown with lace trim. She did not approach and hug me like I wish she would, she stayed at a cool distance and looked me up and down trying to decide if she approved of what she saw.

"Another child was found dead," I said without a *hello*.

"I know," she said without emotion. "I saw on the news that she was found in an alleyway an hours drive from here."

"Yes," I said. "I was questioned by the police today. They thought it was suspicious that all four children were attending my class."

My mother raised an eyebrow. " And what did you tell them?" she asked.

I swallowed hard seeing my mother's accusing eyes. "I told them the truth, mother," I told her. "I told them that I knew nothing, could not help them."

"Good," she said after a long pause, "you could not kill anyone."

I smiled but my mother did not. "Where is Clarissa?" I asked.

"Close by," my mother said. With that she turned and left the room.

My mother was never much for conversation, not with me anyhow. I walked from the kitchen into the living room to see Clarissa sitting on the sofa. She raised a hand when I spoke. Clarissa was my sister but to my shame I had feelings for her. She was a lot younger than myself, blonde like my mother had been, attractive like my mother had been. She always dressed like some cheap prossie, today she wore a strap top and Jean hotpants. Her legs were slung over the arms of the sofa, golden brown and smooth, a slice of cheek revealed by the high cut of the hotpants. She was watching some reality show on TV, which one I couldn't say, something with cooking in it, could have been anything.

I coughed nervously. "How are you, Clarissa?" I asked.

"Better than you," she said without tearing her eyes away from the TV.

I fidgeted. "What do you mean?" I asked.

"I hear you were questioned by police," she scoffed.

"Nothing happened," I said to the back of her head.

"Of course it didn't," she said scornfully, "you couldn't kill anyone, you haven't got the balls. Now if they'd arrested you for being a pervert I could understand it.'

"What?"

"I've seen the way you look at me," she commented. "I can read the mind of every man, I know when someone wants to fuck me."

"You're my sister," I protested.

“Yet you still want to put your dick inside me,” she said, “I bet you pull you tiny cock at night dreaming of being between these amazing legs.” With that she ran a manicured hand up a silky thigh.

I turned away quickly, my body hot with guilt. My wife Olivia was standing watching me from the kitchen doorway. My breath caught in my throat and I could feel my face burning with shame. “Olivia,” I said and stepped in to kiss her but she side stepped me.

“I can see how you would want her,” she said matter-of-factly. “But is she young enough?”

A laugh came from behind me, but when I turned Clarissa was gone leaving me and Olivia alone.

“She’s a bitch,” I said, “I think there’s something wrong with her.”

“There’s something wrong with you,” she said.

“Meaning?”

“Nothing,” she said dismissively. “I haven’t got time for you right now.’

“I love you,” I said honestly.

Olivia gave me a stern look. “Whatever,” she said.

Olivia was a beautiful woman and way out of my league. She was blonde and small framed with sharp blue eyes and lips you could become addicted to. We had always had a very active sex life and she had been very adventurous, bondage, necrophilia, sadism, role play, you name it I enjoyed it with my wife. That all changed when our daughter died. The house, once a buzz of activity was suddenly quiet as a tomb. I would sit alone for days rocking back and forth, I couldn't even bear to look at another human being. Then one by one I let people come back into my life, be it out of loneliness or my cognitive self putting itself back together I don't know, but eventually I had my family around me again, as fucked up as it all was it felt good...mostly.

"I don't want us to fight tonight," I told Olivia. "Let's catch a movie."

Olivia laughed. "Yes, that would be amusing."

"What now?"

"Me and you together? Out in public? People laughing at you."

"Why? Because I'm so ugly and you're so damn beautiful? How conceited."

"Never mind," she said shaking her head.

She attempted to walk away but I stepped in front of her. "Just talk to me," I said. "I need this. I need us to connect."

She looked at me, all emotion covered in ice. "What about what I need," she said. And with that she was gone.

I wanted to cry. It had taken a long time to reunite my family and now I thought we were fractured beyond repair. My family seemed to hate me, hard tones and emotionless. I didn't think I could take it much longer. I went back into the kitchen and pulled out a bottle of JD from the cupboard. I poured a tumbler full and took it in one like a shot. I felt the sweet burning sensation at the back of my throat and poured myself another. I was about to swallow that too when I heard something coming from downstairs. I abandoned my drink and slowly opened the cellar door.

"Hello?" I said tentatively. There was no answer but the sounds continued. "Mother? Jacob?"

Nothing.

I began to walk down the steps that led to the cellar. I stepped carefully, darkness closing in on me as I descended. The wooden stairs creaked a warning beneath my feet, *"Stay awayyyyy. Go baaacckkkk."*

As I drew near the bottom of the stairs I could hear a voice, it was muffled but it was clearly that of a child. I rounded the corner at the foot of the stairs and my body seized and refused to breathe.

Beneath a single naked light bulb in the centre of the room sat a small child. She had long blonde hair pulled back in a ponytail, her frightened eyes darted from left to right as if looking for something or someone. She had a balled-up piece of rag stuffed into her mouth and her hands and feet were tied to the wooden chair on which she was sitting. She wore pink panties and a sweater that was torn and contained splashes of red that I knew was blood. Lacerations covered her thighs and I could see bite marks on her neck, the teeth had broken the skin and trickles of blood ran down her supple flesh and soaked into the collar of her sweater. As I moved closer I saw that she was not wearing pink pants at all, she was actually naked below and bleeding, I had been too late to save this child from losing her virginity to a maniac, but I could hopefully save her life.

The girl stopped staring about her as I approached and fixed her eyes on me, when she did so she began to scream through her gag and kick out her skinny legs as far as the binds would allow.

"I'm here to rescue you," I said. "I'm gonna get you out of here."

As I crouched down in front of her to untie her thrashing feet I looked up at her face. Her eyes were full of fear and her features twisted with a mixture of pain and panic, but I still recognised her.

"Linda," I said shocked.

Linda Gregory was a girl from my class, she had been friends with Marilyn Fitzpatrick, they were neighbours, they played together and now whoever was doing it wanted to kill her as he had killed Marilyn. I hesitated, my hands hovering over the ropes that bound Linda feet. *"Had he killed all the children in my house?"* I thought. *"Why is he trying to blame me for this?"*

"Get away from my child!" someone said from the shadows.

I scurried back until I hit my shoulder against the stairs, pain coursing through my neck.

“Who are you?” I said as a man emerged from the shadows.

“Victor, you know me, “ he said.

I watched him walked into the light. He was slim and dark skinned, he wore work jeans, heavy work boots and a plain black t-shirt. His dark hair was pushed back and held there by a blood stained bandana. “I am Abdul,” he told me.

“What are you doing in my home?” I screamed.

The man rolled his eyes. “We’ve met,” he said. “I did a job for you, remember. You couldn’t do it yourself so you asked me.”

“I’ve never asked you for a thing,” I snarled. “I don’t know you and I don’t want to know you. I want you to get the hell out of my house.”

“I cant,” he said smiling. “I have a job to do.”

I was afraid to ask but I heard the words come from my mouth anyway. “What job?”

For the first time I realised that the young girl, Linda Gregory, had stopped screaming she was now looking confused and scared from myself to Abdul and back again.

Abdul coughed to get my attention. "If you don't like the sight of blood why don't you shut your eyes," he said calmly.

"Just let me take the girl," I was almost sobbing now. "I'll let you go, I won't call the police, just let me have the girl."

Abdul hooked his hand under Linda's chin setting her fear alight again. She began a choked scream and thrashed about in her chair but he was too strong for her and held her easily in one strong hand. The other hand dipped into his pocket and withdrew holding a cylindrical vile. He shook the vile and a toothpick popped out in between his fingers. He plucked the toothpick clear of the vile and held it next to Linda head.

"Please don't," I begged. I held my hands up, palms out. "Stop, I implore you. Let me take her."

Abdul grinned widely flashing perfect teeth. "And let you have her for yourself? Not likely."

He took the toothpick and plunged it into Linda's cheek. The girl let out a sound I'd never heard before almost inhuman in its tone. Abdul pushed the toothpick clear through her cheek forcing it through flesh and muscle. With a flick of his wrist he shot another toothpick out of the vile. He raised it to Linda cheek as he'd done with the first and, ignoring my pleas to stop pressed it into the soft flesh of her cheek. Linda jerked her head as Abdul pushed in the second toothpick, she threw her head towards him and for a split second he lost his grip on the toothpick and the force of her head drove the toothpick into the palm of Abdul's hand. He shouted out in pain and jumped away from Linda.

I knew that I could not save her but I needed to get to a phone and call the police before Abdul could escape. While he was preoccupied with his hand I leapt to my feet and ran up the cellar stairs, curses followed me like hunting dogs but I kept running. I met my wife half way up and she scowled at me.

"Where are you going in a hurry?" she snapped.

"Get out of here," I shot at her. "Run."

I threw open the door at the top of the stairs and part fell into the kitchen and headed for the living room where my phone sat on the small side table. As I snatched it up and headed for the front door, my sister,

Clarissa, appeared from nowhere. I pushed past her ignoring the fact that she was just in her underwear.

‘Where are you going?" she called after me as I exited the house. "I thought you wanted to fuck."

"Get out of there," I called as I dialled the police. "Run, get out."

I dialled the number, not 999 but the station where I had been questioned. They answered on the third ring.

"I need to talk to Detective Mason," I snapped at the operator.

"What is your emergency, sir?" she asked.

"Murder," I said breathlessly. "Give me Detective Mason."

The woman hesitated clearly concerned by what I had said. A few long seconds later she spoke again. "Wait one moment, sir."

The next voice I heard was also female, but she sounded younger. "Hello, Detective Alison Carter."

"I want Detective Mason," I said through gritted teeth. "I spoke to him this morning. It's urgent, I need Detective Mason."

There was a silence that lasted so long I thought I'd lost connection. When she did speak again it was with confusion. “Sir, I’m sorry but we don’t have a Detective Mason.”

The phone dropped from my hand and I sank to my knees.

Part Two

Detective Daria Bassick stood in front of *the board.* It contained four photos of the four children who had been found murdered in the past year. Other photos adorned the board too, none were suspects...yet. They included people from the children’s lives with coloured thread leading from one photo to the next representing any connections that they may have had to the victims. Daria pondered *the board*, going over all the information that she had memorised from the files. She mentally sorted the information into categories and put them into sets and subsets before analysing the information all without writing anything down.

It didn’t matter how many times she went over the information in her mind she could not disregard the teacher that was connected to all four children, but his interview this morning had revealed nothing. Sure the guy seemed a raving lunatic, but that did not make him guilty. She had tried leaving him alone for an hour, an old cop trick that let the suspect sit it out, but all it resulted in doing is giving him time to...talk to himself?

She could not see any other connections, however, maybe the father of the first victim, Samantha Henshaw, who had known two of the other children as well as his daughter, but she had spoken to him herself and she knew in her heart of hearts that he was not the killer.

Daria was about to call it a night when Detective Kenwright entered the room. He nodded a hello and dropped a manila envelope onto one of the desks. "Just a present for Jo," he said with a smile. He turned to leave and then his head snapped round and he stood staring at *the board.*

Daria gave him a deep frown. "Something the matter Kenwright?" she asked.

"What the fuck?". he said approaching *the board.* He prodded the teachers photograph with his finger.

"What the fuck is he doing on your board?" he said staring at the photo.

"Victor Mason?" she said. "What about him? He's the teacher at the school of the victims."

Kenwright tore his eyes away from the photo and gave Daria a look so intense that it gave her butterflies, and not in a good way. "What's the matter?" Daria asked. "I'm getting a feeling that you know something important."

"You got the address?" Kenwright said already leaving.

"Yes," Daria said following. "What's going on?"

Kenwright insisted that Daria drive and drive quickly. While she drove he punched a number into his mobile and spoke with urgency, then, as soon as he clicked of one call, he made a second call. As he clicked off the second call he threw his phone against the dashboard making Daria jump and the car swerve.

"Fucking sonofabitch!" he shouted.

"What the fuck is wrong?" Daria asked waving an apology to a driver that she nearly drove off the road. "What were the phone calls about."

“You know I was transferred, right?” Kenwright asked.

“Yes,” she said. “Last year?”

Kenwright nodded. “And for a year I’ve been sharing a seat with my ass,” he said. “I was transferred here because I had too much light on me after I put away a murderer.

“Victor Mason?” she asked.

“The man is not Victor Mason,” Kenwright said. “I knew him from before I came to London, his name is Daniel Ricliffe. He killed his entire family, his mother, his sister, his wife and his young daughter, Amanda.”

“I remember that case,” Daria said. “Didn’t he rape his sister and daughter?”

“Yes,” Kenwright said sadly. “Unfortunately he’d been doing it for years and even his wife covered it up cause she was scared of him. She had every right to be because, apparently, she confronted him and he went crazy torturing and killing the whole family. He even had sex with the corpses.”

“Jesus Christ. And the phone calls?”

“One was to the prison where he was sent and the other to the psychiatric hospital where he was transferred after convincing a court that he was crazy. There was a fuck up with the paperwork, the prison thought he was at the hospital, the hospital thought he was back in prison and somewhere in between he was released.”

“Fuck,” Daria said instantly stepping on the gas. “Do you think he killed the missing kids?”

“Before I saw the photo of Daniel Ricliffe I never pieced anything together, but now I think about it, each victim looked like his daughter, even the young boy had long blonde hair.”

“Please let Marilyn Fitzpatrick be the last,” she said.

I sat on the curb, my head was spinning, images playing inside my head like some nightmarish slide show. The bodies of my mother, my wife, my sister, my daughter; my darling daughter, Amanda. I saw her now in my mind, playing in the park, her little dress fluttering about her thighs as she ran screaming with delight; cut to her bedroom, her lying beneath me screaming, my hand over her mouth trying to smother the sound, her small delicate body crushed by my weight; cut to my sister, my beautiful sister seeing me with Amanda, threatening to tell my wife, I couldn't have her do that; cut to my sister tied to the bed, her nakedness exciting me, stirring my sexual being; cut to my wife crying and screaming, the accusations that I didn't love Amanda, the name calling, the threats to call the police and then...blood, gallons of blood, dear god it was everywhere.

I covered my face with my hands and felt a sharp stabbing pain just below my right eye. I withdrew my hands and examined them, a toothpick was protruding from the palm of my hand.

"I'm telling you we need units at the address of Victor Mason," Detective Kenwright yelled into the phone. "Get every available man there now!" He clicked off the phone and let out a cry of frustration. "Are we anywhere near our destination?" he snapped.

"We're ten minutes away," Daria said. "I'm driving as fast as I can."

“I’m sorry, okay,” Kenwright said. “I’m just scared that he’ll do it again, maybe he already has another child, maybe he realises we’re closing in and he’s leaving, or left already.”

“We’ll get the fucker,” Daria said, “I’ll make sure of that.”

Daria swerved through the traffic to a symphony of blaring car horns, but she ignored everything but the road. She could not believe that she had been so stupid. She had had the killer in a room, she had seen his strange behaviour, talking to himself, or rather to a figment of his own imagination. And what of that, was it a coping mechanism? Was there some deeper psychological condition? Was he just a crazy bastard? The more she thought about it the more she pushed the car forward, a tightness of panic forming in the centre of her chest.

I moved back inside the house. My sister greeted me. Now she was naked, her perfectly formed body covered in blood, her soft skin marred by razor blade cuts.

"Daniel, fuck me," she said. "I want you inside me."

I moved out of her way as she advanced. My throat tight, tears blurring my vision. I moved into the kitchen, my mother blocked the cellar door, her tongue down the throat of Jacob, her lover. He pulled out of the kiss and looked at me. He grinned and his hand pulled open my mother's dress and cupped her naked drooping breast.

"I'm going to fuck her while you watch," he sneered.

I slammed the heel of my right hand into the side of my head. "Go away, go away, go away," I repeated. My body shaking with anguish.

I reached out my hand passing through them both and gripped the cellar door handle yanking it open. I stepped through the door and made my way down the stairs into the cellar. My wife stood at the foot of the stairs a cold hard look in her eyes.

"How can you do this?" she asked. "You like fucking babies? You're not a real man, are you?" With that she opened her mouth wide and cock roaches and beetles ran out from inside her, running down her chin and neck and over her breasts, her dress beginning to darken with blood.

I hesitated then closed my eyes and ran through her, my sobs audible now. The child was still sitting tied to the chair, her eyes half closed, passing out from the pain, a toothpick protruding from her cheek, her thighs black with dry blood. I ran towards her and threw myself to my knees and untied her feet. "I'm getting you out of here," I said. "I'll take you to a hospital, you'll be okay."

I stood to free her hands when something moved out of the shadows. When I saw Abdul I screwed up my eyes and wished him away, but when I opened them again he was still there. "I know you're unreal," I sobbed. "You are in my head, you're not real."

Abdul laughed. "I'm in your head," he said, "but I am very real. You brought me to life to do what you could not." He raised his right hand in which he held a large hunting knife. "But why am I Asian?" he asked puzzled. "Is this what a killer is to you you racist fuck?"

“Get out of my head!” I screamed. “I don’t need you. Fuck off.” I slammed the heel of my hand into the side of my head again.

Abdul laughed. “If you really want me gone then you’ll have to learn to do things for yourself. Here.”

I looked down to see the hunting knife in my hand. I screamed and threw the knife to the floor, it clattered at the feet of Abdul, but when I looked down the knife was still in my hand.

“You have to learn to do things for yourself,” Abdul said again. “Now kill the little tramp. Slit her delicate throat.”

My body seemed to work independently from my mind. I tried to resist but my free hand reached out and grabbed the hair of Linda Gregory and jerked back her head. The skin of her neck revealed itself to me so clean and fresh like the skin of a peach. I spun the knife in my hand and raised it to slice the peach.

My body spasmed at the same time that two loud bangs shattered my ears. The knife fell from my hand and I dropped to my knees, pain engulfed my body but as I slumped to the cellar fall that pain gave way to a calm and my body relaxed and for the first time in years I felt at peace. My eyes flicked and I saw shadows move toward me. Voices, one male, one female spoke to the girl in hushed gentle tones.

"You'll be safe now," I said, then...nothing.

"Is he dead?" Daria said as she lifted the child into her arms.

Kenwright stood and looked down at Daniel Ricliffe. "The bastard got lucky," he said. "We killed him."

The Knock Knock Box

The Knock Knock Box

Knock

It was the bigger of the five, Kenny Logan, that pushed Simon Mullen first, a wide, rotund boy of fifteen, with a bolder of a head that sat directly on his shoulders, not a neck to be found. He always wore his school tie as a huge knot with a small piece of material trailing from the bottom as if he was being strangled by a blue and burgundy striped mouse.

Kenny grunted three times as he struck Simon's chest with his spade like hands in a powerful shove. 'You're a fucking prick, Mullen,' he said, 'a piece of fucking shit, in fact, I'd rather be friends with shit than even look at you.' The other boys laughed. 'You gonna cry, Mullen?' Kenny said. 'You gonna cry to your daddy? Oh, that's right, you haven't got a daddy, have you? Even your daddy couldn't fucking stand you, you'll have to cry to your step daddy then.'

Another boy stepped forward. James Wilkinson was tall and pipe cleaner thin with a hook nose and sunken eyes that crossed slightly. James would have been perfect to be the victim of bullies but for him being a brown belt in karate.

'His step dad is too busy being drunk and fucking his mum to give a fucking shit about this arse,' James laughed. Then, taking a step back, launched a kick that struck Simon mid-chest and sent him backwards into the wall of the science lab. Simon's head snapped back and made a hollow thud as it struck the brick work.

Simon's hand went immediately to the back of his head where he found a fresh lump already there. A second blow to the stomach sent Simon to the floor where he lay gasping for breath.

The third boy, Seymour Harris, planted a sharp toe poke kick to Simon's ribs. 'Only cool kids go to this school,' Harris said. 'You should stay home and never come back.'

The second Harris kick caught Simon in the balls and he involuntarily curled up into a ball, pain climbing up through his groin and into his stomach. His hands covered his face to prevent the bullies seeing his tears and to muffle the soft sobs.

All five boys gathered around the whimpering Simon and one by one they spat down on him; his blazer and torn grey school trousers were peppered with spittle and a fat green slug of a gob slid down Simon's neck and into his shirt. Simon heard the boys laugh and eventually walk away, he lay there for a good ten minutes, his body painfully shaking as he cried.

Simon did not reach home until after dark. The lights were on and he could hear his mother shouting from the kitchen. His step-father, Larry Crust, answered with shouts of his own, angry shouts tinged with drunkenness. Simon entered the house and dropped his bag and coat in the closet and crept towards the stairs. As he began to ascend he heard his step-father's voice behind him.

'Hey, kid, where do you think you're going?'

'To my room,' Simon said without turning.

'Come here,' Larry demanded.

'I'm tired.'

'Get your fucking ass here, and I mean now.'

Simon turned and saw his step-father at the foot of the stairs looking up at him. He was dressed in a grubby white vest with sweat pants, his hair was brown and wild like a hurriedly made nest, he was dirty shaven and he smelled of alcohol. Larry looked Simon over until his eyes focussed on Simon's ripped trousers.

'What the fuck happened to those?' Larry said angrily.

Simon bowed his head. 'I fell over,' he said quietly.

'You fell over? Get the fuck out of here, don't you lie to me. You've been fighting haven't you?'

Simon shook his head. 'No,' he said. He wasn't lying, a fight was a two-way confrontation and there was no two-way anything what had happened to him.

'You, boy, are a fucking liar,' Larry said seizing Simon by the arm.

'Let go,' Simon protested.

Larry jerked Simon down the last few stairs. 'Don't you lie to me. I want to know what happened to those trousers, I'm not fucking made of money.'

As Simon tried to pull away Larry grabbed him by the hair and slapped the boy's face. 'What happened, fucker? Don't lie again.'

‘Let me go,’ Simon shouted, as he felt the hair tearing from his head. ‘Mum, please help me.’

‘Your mum can’t help you, shit for brains,’ Larry said slapping him twice more.

Simon’s face burned with each slap and his head ached where Larry had a tight grip.

‘Leave him alone, you sonofabitch.’

Simon twisted to see his mother come from the kitchen. His mum had been beautiful at one time but now she seemed haggard like a crack addict on some sleazy TV cop show, only it wasn’t crack that had blotched her once radiant skin or darkened her once blonde hair, it was a life with a scumbag like Larry.

‘Let him go,’ she said heading for her husband.

‘Stay out of this, Chrissie’ Larry said, turning his anger towards Simon’s mother.

Chrissie grasped Larry by the arm that held Simon’s hair with one hand and punched Larry in the shoulder with the other.

Larry released Simon and with one fluid motion back handed Chrissie across the face. As his mother fell Simon lashed out at Larry kicking him in the shin. ‘Motherfucker!’ Simon yelled.

Larry spun and went at Simon growling like some beast.

'Get out, Simon,' his mother said. 'Go.'

Simon ran for the door, flung it open and ran into the street. Simon began to run. He could hear his step-father close behind him, but Simon was young and his father was drunk. Simon made his advantage pay, he sprinted down the street pushing himself to outrun the monster that was his step-father, and he kept running until his legs felt like jelly and the burning in his chest reached up his throat and threatened to choke him.

Simon stopped, bent double and placed his hands on his knees, he breathed deeply trying to get himself under some sort of control. When he had calmed, he realised how cold it had become, he had left his jacket at the house and now he began to shiver. He knew that he could not go back to the house unless he wanted a beating, so he had to find somewhere to get out of the cold. Simon knew that he was close to the park and in that park he knew that there was a large shed owned by the grounds keeper, he also knew that the grounds keeper kept a key to the shed under a large stone by the shed door, perhaps he could keep warm there, at least until he decided what he should do.

With renewed hope Simon headed for the park. He paused by the entrance and looked beyond the gate. The park was pitch black, the trees hissed throwing shadows into shadows. With a nervous swallow Simon entered the park and followed the path that he knew led to the shed. As the dark closed around him Simon became scared. The smell of rotting garbage and urine filled the cold night air, the wind whistling through the trees seemed to speak to him in the voice of the bullies – *'We hate you, Mullen.' 'You're shiiiiiiit, Mullen.' 'No one likes you, Simon Mullen.'* The cold seemed to snatch at his skin like the icy hand of his step-father.

Simon was happy when he reached the shed. He crouched and felt along the wall of the shed until his fingers fell upon a large stone; he lifted it and found the key. Simon then ran his fingers down the edge of the door until he found the lock and slid the key into it turning it until he heard a satisfying click. He pulled the door open and was about to step inside when he heard a noise behind him.

Simon froze.

He waited, his ears attuned to every sound. Then someone grabbed him from behind, two strong hands throwing him to the ground. Simon cried out as someone climbed on top of him. He could feel their hot sour breath against his face, their weight pinning him down. Simon struggled, trying to push the stranger away, the rough hessian feel of the man's coat scratching Simon's hands.

'Keep still,' the man said. 'I like you, I want to show you that I like you.'

'Get off me, please,' Simon cried out. 'Leave me alone, leave me alone.'

'You're in my park,' the man said, 'and you have to pay the fee, and the fee is…'

Simon felt cold wet lips on his neck, the scratch of a dirty shaven face against his. He closed his eyes and prayed for someone to save him as a calloused hand forced its way inside Simon's trousers. Simon panicked, what happened next was automatic, like a force guiding his actions. Simon reached out his hand sweeping it side to side until he found the stone that had hidden the shed key. In one swift movement

Simon picked up the stone and smashed it against the head of his assailant. The man howled in pain and rolled off the top of Simon. At once Simon was on his feet and running once more. The man cried out, but Simon did not stop to pay attention, he ran blindly through the dark not caring about anything but putting distance between him and the man who had attacked him.

When Simon had been running for a while he began to pay attention, his eyes were adjusting to the dark and his body was responding to auditory clues, turning towards the hum of traffic. Within minutes Simon saw street lights ahead and after several more minutes he found himself at the park exit, but this was not the gate where he had entered, this was unfamiliar, the streets beyond the exit were unfamiliar too. He had never seen this part of town, strange shops without names, dark and foreboding, all but one.

The Curio Shop was a glass fronted establishment with a large blue neon sign above it. It looked like no other shop Simon had ever seen. Strange artefacts sat on display in the window, a teddy bear with different coloured eyes and an arm missing. A doll with the mouth sewn shut, a wooden box with carvings in the sides and sealed with a tiny gold padlock. Simon didn't know why but he went inside.

The shop was brightly lit and filled with objects as strange as there had been in the window. Simon saw a painting of a man in a coffin and a woman kissing the corpse on the mouth; there was a soft toy hedgehog with nails as spines; several other dolls like the one in the window but with various deformities.

'Can I help you?'

Simon jumped and spun around.

An old man emerged from the back of the shop, he was as curious as the dolls on the shelves. He was old with thick grey hair that fell to his slender shoulders, his skin was wrinkled around the eyes one of which was bright blue the other was obscured by a patch. The wrinkles continued around the mouth that held a soft smile that Simon saw as genuinely friendly. The man wore an oversized shirt and loose slacks, his feet slipped into brown leather sandals.

'Can I help you?' the man said again.

'No…no, I'm sorry to disturb you,' Simon said. He turned to leave.

'You didn't disturb me,' said the old man. 'In fact, I'm glad of the company. Would you like some tea, perhaps a sandwich? You look hungry.'

Simon froze to the spot. On the one hand, he wanted to run as he'd had enough of people today; on the other hand, he *was* hungry and tired and for some strange reason he did trust the old man.

Sensing his indecision, the old man smiled. 'I forget my manners,' he said, stepping forward and holding out a wrinkled hand. 'My name is Zeek, and yours?'

Simon returned the warm smile with one of his own and took Zeek's hand shaking it tentatively. 'My name is Simon.'

'Please to meet you, Simon, now we are friends. Tea?'

Zeek led the way into the back of the shop behind a beaded curtain. There Simon saw a table with a teapot at its centre and a plate of sandwiches that looked delicious. Zeek motioned for Simon to sit.

Once they had seated and Simon had filled his plate with food, Zeek said, 'So what is the matter?'

‘Matter?’ Simon asked, ‘why would anything be the matter.’

Zeek smiled once more. ‘Don’t be shy,’ he said, ‘you are a young boy out in the cold with no coat. Did someone hurt you?’

Simon couldn’t help but laugh. ‘You could say that.’

Zeek sat back in his chair his gnarled fingers knitted across his stomach. ‘I have time, tell me, please.’

Simon looked up into Zeek’s eyes so soft and friendly. Simon didn’t want to talk, but he did. He did not know why but he started to tell Zeek everything; he told him about the bullies at school and about his step-father at home, he even told him about the man attacking him in the park, and it felt good. Time passed and Simon unburdened himself while Zeek sat and listened, nodding every now and then and never taking his eyes off Simon.

When he was finished, Simon felt spent as if he had run a marathon and he felt his eyes beginning to close. ‘I have to go,’ Simon said. He tried to stand but his legs felt weak and didn’t move properly.

Zeek waved a hand in the air. ‘Sleep, my child,’ he said.

‘No I…’ Simon felt light headed, colours danced in front of his closing eyes.

‘Sleep, my child,’ Zeek said again. ‘Awaken tomorrow and it will be a new beginning.’

And though Simon fought to stay awake he drifted off to sleep.

Knock

Simon awoke with a start. He looked around him, confused. The room that he was in was a small plain room that smelled of liquorice, the bed was warm and comfortable, but where was he? Then his memories began to return from the day before, the bullies beatings, the physicality of his step-father, the man attacking him in the park and the old man. The old man, Zeek. Zeek had been warm and kind and had listened to him, really listened like no one had ever done before. Simon assumed that Zeek had given him a bed for the night.

Simon climbed out of bed and slipped on his shoes. He was about to leave when he noticed a carved wooden box sitting on a table beside the bed along with a note. Simon recognised the box from the one he'd seen in the window the previous evening. It was dark wood and carved on four sides with strange symbols, two circles joined by a cross, a triangle with an M beneath it and what Simon thought looked like two headless, naked women back to back.

Simon picked up the note and read it:

Dear Simon

This is a gift for you. It is a Knock Knock Box and is very special. Just tap the box twice and tell it your problems, it will help you.

It has helped many in the past.

Your friend, Zeek

Simon picked up the box and ran downstairs to thank *his friend*, but the shop was empty. Simon looked everywhere, in the room where they had eaten sandwiches, upstairs where he found a second bedroom and a bathroom, but no Zeek.

Simon looked at his watch, 7.05am, he'd been away from home all night, Larry would be furious. Simon left the shop and headed for the park. From there he managed to find his way back to the shed where he'd been attacked and from there he made his way home.

As he entered the house he was aware of its stillness, a quiet that was unusual for post 8am. Satisfied that his step-father was not in wait, Simon crept upstairs and into his room. He opened the closet and put the *Knock Knock Box* on the floor and covered it in a blanket. Simon stood and grinned down at the gift and his smile widened remembering the note *'Your friend, Zeek'*. Simon felt warm inside and an alien feeling that he never thought he'd feel again – happy.

Simon turned to get ready for school – Larry struck him hard across the face sending him to the floor. Larry gripped Simon by the shirt collar and hoisted him violently to his feet.

Simon's hands went up automatically to protect his face. 'Please don't,' he cried. 'Please, I'm sorry.'

'Where the fuck have you been?' Larry snapped as he struck Simon again. 'Where have you been you little shit?' He pushed Simon hard sending him crashing into his chest of drawers, his model of the Millennium Falcon smashing into thousands of pieces. Larry unfastened his belt and slid it off. 'You'll learn to respect me, boy,' he said advancing.

Simon was defenceless, all he could do was curl up into a ball and wait until it was over.

Larry did not say another word he just lashed out with the belt striking Simon across the back. Simon winced and made a sound like an injured pup. Larry lashed him again, and again, each strike more powerful than the last. Simon's shirt tore, bloody wounds appeared crisscrossing each other across his pale young skin.

It was only when Simon's mother came into the room and began screaming at her husband did he stop, but only to turn his violence on her, but Simon was helpless to do anything about his mother; he simply lay crying and bleeding surrounded by the pieces of his broken toy and listened to his mother's screams.

Who's

Simon got to school three hours late, the pain in his back constantly bringing tears to his eyes which he wiped away with the cuff of his shirt. His English class was in full swing when he got there. He took a seat without explaining his tardiness. The welts on his back screamed as he leaned against the back of his chair. He floated through the lesson without hearing a word, his mind filled with his mother's cries. After class, he moved through the hallways like a ghost unaware of his surroundings.

His next lesson was geography, but Simon knew that he could not face it, so he decided to hide in the lavatory until everyone was in class and then make his way to *The Curio Shop* and see his friend, Zeek. Simon went into the lavatory and locked himself into the second stall. He heard the door open soon after and heard the footsteps of boys entering, whispered voices and soft laughter. Simon sat still and quiet and hoped that they would leave soon.

'Hey, fuck face.'

Simon looked up to see the face of James Wilkinson peering down at him over the top of the next stall.

'What you doing, Mullen?' he said, 'jerking off?'

'Is that filthy cunt jerking off in there?' said Kenny Logan from outside the stall. 'Hey, Mullen, are you spunking your pants?' he shouted banging on the stall door with his fist.

Simon didn't say a word, but even if he wanted to his throat was too dry and tight with fear.

Kenny pounded on the door again while James laughed down at him. 'Come out, Mullen, you fucking pervert. Don't make me kick the fucking door in or it'll be worse for you.'

Simon stayed rooted, terror cursing through him.

'Mullen, I'll give you three,' Kenny said through the door. 'There won't be a four.'

Simon slowly got to his feet and unlocked the door. As soon as the lock clicked the door was kicked open and Kenny dragged Simon out of the stall.

'We're not finished from yesterday, are we, boys?' Kenny said.

James Wilkinson and Seymour Harris grinned from either side of their leader.

'Please let me go,' Simon said. 'I just want to go home; I don't feel well.'

'Ahhh, he doesn't feel well,' Harris said with a laugh. 'Is it your stomach?' He punctuated the word *stomach* with a vicious blow to Simon's stomach.

Simon doubled over his arms across his midriff.

James grabbed Simon by his hair and lifted his head. 'Yeah, he looks ill,' he said spitting in Simon's face.

Kenny stepped forward and pushed Simon against one of the sinks.

'Don't,' Simon said.

Kenny looked at Simon, his head to one side. 'Don't?' he said. 'Don't? Why what the fuck are you going to do about it, get your step-daddy to beat us up, word is he's too busy beating the fuck out of you and your mum.'

'Hey, Kenny,' Harris called from the third stall. 'There's still a shit floating in this one.'

Kenny grinned. 'Really?'

'Don't,' Simon pleaded, 'please don't.'

'Get him, boys.'

The three boys grabbed Simon, Kenny seized his legs and James and Harris taking his arms. Simon struggled trying to free himself, but there was three against one and all stronger than he was. The boys hoisted Simon in the air and carried him to the toilet. Simon could see a large stool floating in a yellow lake, faeces smeared around the pan. He kicked and struggled but that only resulted in the boys holding him tighter.

'Don't please,' Simon was openly crying now, his heart almost bursting through his chest. 'I'll do anything, don't do this.'

The boys upended Simon and lowered his head into the toilet bowl.

'Open wide,' Kenny said laughing.

The floating faeces pushed against Simon's face breaking apart and flowing into his nostrils and mouth. Simon tried to spit but the shit and piss water forced its way into his throat.

The boys lowered Simon down and stood back as Simon pulled his head from the pan and vomited over himself.

‘Fuck, man, you look fucking disgusting.’

‘And Jesus you smell…’

‘Like shit?’ Kenny said, sending all three of them into reams of laughter. ‘Let’s go, I’ve had enough of this fucker.’

After they left Simon went to one of the sinks. His reflection in the mirror brought fresh tears. Shit was smeared all over his face and in his hair and down his shirt, vomit ran down his chin and joined the brown stain on his from. Simon washed his face and his hair in the sink; he planned to steal a shirt from the changing rooms while the others took PE. When he’d finished he looked more like his old self, but it didn’t matter how much he rinsed his mouth he could not get rid of the taste of shit.

There

Simon sat in his room, the faecal taste still in his mouth even though he had brushed his teeth for what seemed like a million times. Tears rolled down his face and his thoughts wandered to a documentary he had seen on TV about killing yourself. He'd seen where people had tied sheets to beams and hung themselves and taken pills, and Simon wondered what it would be like to die.

He had left school and ran off to try and talk to his friend, Zeek, at *The Curio Shop*, but it didn't matter how many times he ran around the park he could not find the gate that led him to the shop, it was like that particular exit did not exist anymore. After he had circled the park several times Simon had given up and gone home and now sat in his room, heartbroken.

With Zeek gone he had no one, no one who truly cared, no one to talk to, then he remembered Zeek's note and what it had said about *The Knock Knock Box* – *'tap it twice and tell it your problems, it will help you...'*

Simon retrieved the box from the closet and sat it on his bed. He stared at it for several long minutes before shrugging. 'Fuck it, what can it hurt,' he said. He ran his fingers over the carvings feeling the smooth wood and then nervously began to talk. He felt foolish at first, but then, as with when he had talked to Zeek, the hurt just came out. He spoke not just about recent events but found himself talking about everything that had happened, from the day Larry had walked into their lives, the screams he had heard coming from his mother's bedroom, the beating he himself had received, the bullies at school, Kenny and his goons tying him to a fence with wire, locking him in a garage car pit…everything came out; the name calling, the violence, the humiliation.

When Simon had finished he felt lighter, unburdened. He didn't feel silly at all, and, he felt that the box had really listened. That night Simon slept the deepest sleep he had ever slept, a calm nightmare free sleep with the box held close.

DEATH

Kenny Logan, James Wilkinson and Seymour Harris sat around the camp fire drinking beers and laughing at what they had done to Simon Mullen.

'Did you see his face?' Kenny laughed, 'fucking shit and piss all in his hair, that cunt's never gonna get rid of the smell.'

'Fucking too right,' Harris said, taking a long swallow of beer. 'His stupid step-dad probably beat the fuck out of him for going home like that.'

'Beat the *shit* out of him you mean,' James said.

All three rolled on the ground laughing.

'I'll be surprised if he ever comes back to school,' Kenny said.

'Hope he does,' James said, 'so we can fuck with him some more.'

'Fuck with him til he breaks,' Harris added. 'Find that tosser swinging from the basketball hoop in the yard with a note pinned to his chest.'

Kenny spat out his beer with a laugh. 'Dear Mummy, I've been such a fucking loser I wanted to end it all and make people happy.' Kenny knocked back his beer and threw his bottle watching it explode against the trunk of a tree.

James looked behind him. 'What was that?'

'What was what?' Kenny asked.

James scanned the trees before turning back to the fire. 'I heard something.'

'Prick,' Harris said, spitting beer onto the fire and listening to it hiss.

'You been watching too much *Blair Witch*,' Kenny scoffed.

James was suddenly jerked backwards into the dark, his screams echoing through the wood.

'What the fuck?' Harris said scrambling to his feet.

The two remaining boys began to run, they had no plan of escape just to get the fuck out of there. Harris could feel his heart beating against his rib cage, his breath was quick and rasping, looking behind him every few seconds – panic 101.

He could not see where he was going; the moon was a slither and what fragment of light there was was shut out by the canopy of the trees. He could feel the long grass snatching at his ankles like tiny hands, tree branches scratching at his face as sharp as witch's nails. Then the cold came, not the cold of the night air but the cold of a malevolent presence, something terrifying and then…

Kenny heard the screams as he made his way quickly towards what he knew was the road that would lead him home. He could have called after Harris and showed him the way but he had a plan and it had worked. He had followed Harris for a hundred yards or so and then changed direction quickly, he hoped that whatever had gotten James back at the camp fire would go after Harris and give him time to escape, and bingo. Harris had been the perfect decoy.

As Kenny neared the road he slowed and listened, he could hear nothing but the *swish* of traffic just beyond the tree line. Kenny chuckled to himself and made his way towards the road. He would go into the school the next day and have a great story – the boy who escaped a killer.

Suddenly he was pulled back, not by a man but by some kind of force. Kenny slammed into a tree trunk, pain shooting through his spine. His body was pushed up the tree until he was ten feet off the ground, his body pinned there by the same invisible force that had pulled him backwards.

'Let me go,' Kenny shouted into the dark, 'let me go, please.'

'Let me gooooooooooo,' a voice whispered. *'Pleeeeaaassssse.'*

The night mist rose and started to spin in front of Kenny's eyes forming itself into a ball; from that ball appeared a face, pale and savage with hollow eyes and dagger like teeth.

Kenny began to scream, a shrill sound of a small girl.

The face rushed at Kenny as he cried out and he peed himself. The face passed through him, but that's when the pain began. He felt a burning in his feet, then a searing pain as if they were on fire. Kenny looked down to see his boots and socks disintegrate and the skin of his feet tear and fold back on itself. Kenny yelled out and tried to struggle, tried to free himself from whatever was holding him, but he could not move.

The skin pulled back over his ankles and tore away from his calves, his delicate muscle laid bare. Kenny went into shock, the excruciating pain driving him insane. The flesh continued to peel away from his body, from his hips, stomach and chest. Blood poured from his nose and he vomited blood onto the leafy ground below. The flesh tore away from his neck and finally his face. Then his bones began to snap one by one like dry twigs, his eyes were pushed from his head, sliding down his face and dropping like bloody gobstoppers. Finally, his face was pushed in on itself, his skull caving, the tiny bullies brain mashed against the tree trunk.

Simon sat at the breakfast table watching the news. The news reporter was pretty with a solemn expression. She stood talking directly to the camera, Simon's school in the background.

'Behind me,' the reporter said, 'is the school where the three murdered boys attended. The school is closed today while teachers and pupils alike mourn the death of Kenny Logan, James Wilkinson and Seymour Harris who were found skinned and mutilated in woods close to where I now stand.'

'Not everyone is mourning,' Simon said to himself, although he had to admit he was shocked. 'Some of us are very happy indeed.'

The news reporter continued. Kenny Logan was found by a walker who reported it to the police and is now in the hospital suffering from shock. While investigating Kenny Logan's death two more bodies were found in the same horrifying state as that of their friend.

'We spoke to the head mistress Miss Penny Blind who was too distraught to be interviewed on camera but gave us this statement:

'Kenny, James and Seymour will be sorely missed by all. They were not only good students, but good and popular human beings. Kind, generous and...'

Simon turned off the TV unable to listen to anymore of the bullshit. He finished his breakfast and was about to leave the kitchen when his step-father walked in.

'No school today so you can do chores around the house,' he snapped.

'I was going…'

'I don't give a flying fuck where you were going,' Larry cut in. 'You'll do the cleaning, you little shit, you hear me? And do it right or you'll get my belt again.'

Simon bowed his head. 'Yes,' he said sadly.

'I'll be in the garage,' Larry said, 'don't fucking disturb me.'

Simon sighed as Larry walked out and headed for the garage.

Larry entered the garage by the side door and locked it behind him. He flicked on the light and cracked open a beer from a small table top fridge and settled down in a soft leather armchair. The garage was Larry's man cave, a big two car affair with tools that lined three walls, they sat on shelves or hung on hooks, drills and sanders, nail guns and electric saws, and tools of every size to fit any job. Larry was proud of his collection especially the power tools.

Larry slugged down the beer and reached under his chair and retrieved a tattered copy of *Hustler XXX.* Larry flipped to the ear marked page where barely legal girls posed in school uniform touching themselves.

'Oh yeah, baby,' Larry said, unzipping himself and pulling his already stiff cock free.

A noise.

Larry hurriedly pushed his cock back into his pants and stashed the magazine back under the chair. 'Hello, Simon, is that you?' He listened for a while before relaxing and reaching again for the magazine.

A noise stopped him again.

Larry got out of the chair and tried to open the door, but it wouldn't open. He rattled the door twisting the handle this way and that but the door was stuck fast.

'What the hell?' he said to himself. 'Simon, if this is you I'm gonna fucking beat you senseless,' he shouted. He tried the door again, but nothing. 'Hey, let me out,' he called out.

The tools began to clatter on the shelves and on their hooks; the light began to flutter on and off.

'Fuck, an earthquake,' Larry said a little scared.

He was about to settle back in his chair and ride it out when a chisel spun of the shelf and buried itself into Larry's thigh.

'Jesus Christ,' he wailed. He pulled the chisel free and held his hand over the deep wound. 'Let me out,' he shouted again. 'Someone, help.'

A screwdriver flew like it had been shot from a bow and stabbed Larry in the shoulder. He spun in confusion trying to see who was attacking him. Another screwdriver embedded itself into Larry's knee, the pain ripping through him causing the fear and confusion to escalate.

He hobbled to the garage door and clawed at it desperate to escape, his fingernails breaking, ripping back the skin on his fingers. A hammer struck his head, a wrench struck his hip. And then a whirring sound caught his attention. Larry turned to see his electric saw lift off its hook and sail across the garage towards him. Larry raised his hands to protect himself but the saw made easy work of those, scattering fingers across the garage floor and then driving itself into Larry's face. Blood sprayed the walls and ceiling and Larry fell to the floor, dead, as the saw spun to a halt.

Colin Barry wiped his nose on the sleeve of his dirty jacket and stared at passers-by from his hidey hole in the bushes. He waited, eating the sandwiches that he'd found in the bin and a can of coke left behind on a bench. He waited until the light went from the sky and the park became the dark sanctum that he loved. It had been two weeks since he'd gotten some action, that was a sixteen-year-old girl in a wheelchair walking her dog; she had been easy, hardly any struggle at all and of course she couldn't run away.

His only regret is that he'd had to kill the dog as it's yapping could have attracted unwanted attention.

Now he wanted something that was more of a challenge; the boy from a few nights ago had been feisty, he rubbed the lump on his head where he'd hit him with a stone.

Colin watched people as they took their short cuts until he saw a woman alone. He looked around but there was no one else in sight. Colin crept out of his hiding place and followed her at a distance, then, when he thought it was safe, he raced up behind her and grabbed her by the shoulders.

'Come on, darling,' he said, spinning her around.

Colin let out a high-pitched shriek and stumbled backwards. The face of the woman was a pale skull and she hissed at him as she approached. Colin tried to run but something glued him to the spot. He crossed himself and uttered a prayer as the woman's skeletal fingers gripped his collar.

All at once Colin was lifted off his feet and thrown through the air. When he landed he was impaled on the park fence, his body limp and lifeless.

Simon made his mother hot tea with lemon just how she liked it and sat beside her on the couch and held her hand. Their eyes were fixed on the TV and neither of them spoke, neither of them knowing what to say, but Simon somehow knew everything was going to be okay. The bullies were dead, his step-father was dead, Simon had his mother back; he'd also seen a story of a tramp that was found impaled on a spiked fence in the park and Simon knew that that was the man who had attacked him, it all made sense. He had talked to *The Knock Knock Box* and somehow it had made everything alright.

When his mother eventually turned off the TV and said goodnight Simon ran upstairs. He wanted to get rid of the box before anything else happened. He raced into his bedroom, but his bedside cabinet was bare, the box was gone.

Celebrity Baby

Celebrity Baby

Awards

Belinda Ross stood centre stage, the *Best Actress in a Dramatic Role* award held aloft, enjoying the applause and adulation of her peers. 'Thank you,' she said above the cacophony of whoops and cheers, 'thank you so much.' Belinda beamed and waited for the noise to die down. 'I could stand here,' she continued, 'and give you a long list of thank yous to this person and that person, but truth is, those people know who they are so thanks. However, I have something more important to impart. I have an announcement for you lovely people. You may have seen in the gutter press, photos of me in Morocco dressed in a gorgeous Gucci bikini. The headlines were not kind, saying I had gained a lot of weight, the *Daily Mail* going so far as to call me *Bloated Belinda*…'

A thin ripple of laughter ran through the theatre.

'Well, the jokes on you, suckers. The truth is…' Belinda paused for dramatic effect. 'I'm pregnant,' she announced.

The crowd burst into applause once more, shouts of *'Congratulations'* and '*How wonderful'* rang out as well as a media shout of, *'Who's the father?'*

Truth was, Belinda Ross had been dating TVs new hunk, Glen Coletti, runner up of the *X Factor*, contestant on *Strictly Come Dancing* (he was forced to drop out because of a serious toe injury) and winner of *I'm A Celebrity Get Me Out of Here*, for six months now.

Glen Coletti was in the audience watching the spectacle and not believing what he was hearing.

'Congratulations,' whispered actress Lacey Turner from beside him.

Glen looked at the floor. 'Errr, thanks,' he mumbled.

An hour later Belinda Ross sat in the back of a limousine heading back to her London apartment at The Music Box at Southwalk, her mobile phone stuck to her ear. Glen Coletti sat across from her desperate to talk about the announcement but she had been constantly talking to callers since leaving the awards.

‘No, for Christ sake,’ she was saying into the phone, ‘how can the baby possibly be yours? We didn’t even sleep together. I can’t get pregnant just by you looking at me, no matter how macho you think you are.’ Belinda looked at Glen and mouthed, *Danny Dyer*. ‘Dan, Dan, I have another call coming through I have to go.’ Belinda immediately cut off the one call and took the other. ‘Hello? Ah, Jane McDonald if I live and breathe, how are you darling?’ Again Belinda looked at Glen, this time sticking her fingers down her throat. ‘Well, thank you, darling…yes of course I’m delighted…yes, I would love to talk about it on *Loose Women*. Okay, I’ll have Francine to call in the morning to set it up…okay, bye darling, kisses.’ Belinda clicked off the call, ‘Bitch,’ she said. She then snuggled down in her seat and lay her head back, eyes closed.

‘So?’ Glen said.

‘So, what?’ Belinda said without looking up.

‘When were you going to tell me about the pregnancy?’

Belinda shrugged. ‘I didn’t want to spoil the surprise.’

‘Surprise? You can say that again. You left me with my arse in the breeze,’ he said. ‘It was so humiliating. People patting me on the back and I had to pretend I knew all along. So embarrassing.’

Belinda looked up and laughed. 'This is not about you, this about me.'

'This is about the two of us,' Glen said. 'This is about a family now, I'm not going to be an absent father like mine was, it's devastating for a child, it was for me.'

'You're not on the fucking *X Factor* now you know,' she said. 'I don't need anyone, me and the baby will be just fine, this thing will increase my profile; that reminds me, I must visit Ralph Lauren to see if they have some of those cute tops that show off my baby bump.'

Glen slammed his fist into the leather seat beside him. 'This is my life too goddamnit. I'm the child's father and this is my life too.'

'Maybe it's not,' Belinda said.

'What the fuck?'

The limousine pulled up outside of Belinda's apartment; as she got out she held up a hand to stop Glen from following her. 'Driver?' she said, 'take Mr Coletti home, will you?' She looked coldly at the pained face of Glen Coletti in the back seat. 'Bye, Glen,' she said and turned away.

As the limo pulled away Belinda felt a twinge across her middle, she held her stomach. The baby bump felt bigger than usual and she could have sworn she felt the baby move.

Premiere Party

Belinda Ross was the talk of the room. She had already stolen the limelight on the red carpet dressed as she was in a black Ralph Lauren dress that stretched over her bump and had the word *Baby* written in diamonds across her middle, much to the annoyance of Kristen Stewart who was hoping the night would be all about her and her new movie, *The Bad and The Ugly*.

Now Belinda was making the rounds at the party, martini in one hand and a fan in the other which she used to great affect whenever she wanted attention, which was all the time.

'Are you okay dear?' Dame Judy Dench had asked.

'Would you like a seat?' Bradley Cooper Offered.

Belinda was loving it. She waved delicately at Renee Zellweger, or was it Reese Witherspoon? She could never decide. She blew a kiss to Scarlett Johansson, enticed a kiss on the lips from Tom Cruise, which she made sure was captured by the press, and all the time she talked about the baby. Even Ellen DeGeneres offered baby tips.

Half way through the night she found herself sitting at a table, her head light with too much conversation and gin chatting to Sam Faiers.

'You should get your own show,' Sam was saying. 'I didn't know what to do after *The Only Way Is Essex*, but I thought, "Fuck it, I've had a kid, why not make another reality show, only this time all about me." You should definitely do that.'

'That's not a bad idea, Sam,' Belinda said draining her glass. 'I could film the birth, I bet they'd pay a fortune to film that.'

'They would,' Sam agreed sadly. 'I wish I'd done that.'

'There's enough cunts on *TOWIE* without them seeing yours,' Belinda mumbled into her glass.

'One piece of friendly advice though,' Sam offered. 'You shouldn't be drinking while pregnant.'

'Sam,' Belinda slurred, 'this little fucker is going to be ready to tend bar when it arrives. And anyway, the facts about drink and pregnancy are highly exaggerated. I don't smoke, I exercise four times a week and watch what I eat, I do everything for this thing, I'm not giving up my only vice.'

Sam Faiers rolled her eyes and excused herself.

Belinda watched her leave before sipping from her glass. 'Interfering bitch,' Belinda spat. 'My baby show is gonna kick your skinny ass.'

She stood up from the table a little unsteady on her feet and looked the party over. She sighed heavily as she saw Tom Cruise leaving some blonde slag from *Mission Impossible 7* or was it *8*? She noticed Gerard Butler on the far side of the room, but he was talking to that has been bore Tea Leoni. Then she spotted Hans Greenberg. He wasn't an A lister – yet – but he was a handsome rising star and just starred in the new Steven Spielberg epic alongside Denzel Washington. He parted company with Halle Berry and headed for the door. Quickly Belinda cut through the crowd, ignoring, for once, everyone who tried to engage her in conversation.

'Hans,' she called, 'Hans, darling.'

Hans Greenberg stopped and looked over smiling. 'Belinda,' he said, 'how are you? How's the baby? Congratulations.'

Belinda looked at his rugged face with its square jaw covered in designer stubble, his perfect cheek bones, his new nose and hypnotic dark eyes. 'Well, I'm feeling a little sick,' she lied. 'The baby you know. Could you possibly give me a ride home?'

Hans fidgeted uncomfortably. 'Oh, errr, of course,' he said, 'my car is out front.'

As they began to leave Kirsten Stewart stepped in front of them.

'Hans,' she said trying on her sultry tone and failing. 'I'm talking to Ron Howard about a new film and he'd like to talk to you about being in it with me, can you spare a few minutes?'

Hans' eyes moved from Kristen to Belinda and back. 'I…'

'Oh,' Belinda moaned stroking her belly.

Hans swallowed a couple of times audibly. 'Sorry, Kristen, I have to get Belinda home.'

Kristen stepped aside reluctantly.

As Belinda passed her, she smiled lopsidedly. 'Goodnight, Kristen,' she said slyly.

A pain suddenly erupted inside of Belinda like a fire. Belinda gritted her teeth and waited for the pain to pass. Something moved inside her, it felt unnatural, like a snake coiling and uncoiling.

Hans looked back at Belinda seeing her ashen face and tortured expression. 'Are you okay?' he asked with genuine concern.

'Fine,' she said, 'I just need you to take me home.

The Apartment

Belinda feigned weakness as Hans Greenberg opened her apartment door and prepared to say goodnight…and it worked too. Hans wrapped his big, strong arms around her and helped her to her bedroom. Once there she pulled him close and kissed him. He did not resist or pull away, but kissed her too, his lips responding to hers, his tongue dancing in her mouth. Belinda knew her strengths, she was attractive and successful, things that attracted men in her business.

Soon she was pulling off his shirt, running her fingers over his bulking chest and chiselled abs. He too had hurried hands, unzipping her dress and watching it fall…to just below her breasts. He looked down at her swollen stomach and hesitated.

Belinda looked down at herself suddenly disgusted with what she saw. She looked enormous, much bigger than how she thought she should look. Was it an optical illusion brought on by her own self-awareness, or was she growing noticeably larger every day?

Belinda wriggled out of the dress, her huge mid-section a physical barrier between her and the up and coming hunk.

'Have you ever had sex with a pregnant woman?' she asked him trying to sound seductive.

No,' he said, his eyes still fixed on the large bump, 'I…I can't say I have.'

'Then this will be your first,' she said.

Hans looked at his watch. Belinda couldn't believe it, the bastard actually looked at his watch. Before he could do anything else Belinda grabbed at the front of his pants. Feeling he was semi hard she squeezed his cock gently. 'Take off my panties,' she said.

Hans was sweating now; his whole being caught in indecision.

Belinda squeezed a little harder feeling him grow more aroused and then, to Belinda's relief, Hans knelt and pulled down her panties.

Once off Belinda awkwardly got to her knees, cursing her pregnancy to herself, secretly hating the unborn child for spoiling this moment. She unzipped Hans' pants and slid them down with his boxer shorts. His penis stuck out like a swollen thumb. She had expected something more impressive, but she thought, *it's the cock of Hans Greenberg, it's like if Brad Pitt had a tiny dick,* she surmised, *you'd still want to suck it, right?*

Belinda ran her tongue the short length of his cock and took it in her mouth, she began to suck, sliding her lips up and down his shaft running her tongue over it's tip, Hans sighing and moaning, his head thrown back, his fingers in her hair. She stopped and looked up at him, every inch – and in some cases, literally *an inch* – a God.

'I want you to fuck me,' she hissed.

'Okay,' he answered casually.

It took them a couple of minutes to hoist Belinda to her feet and then she bent over the best she could and he entered her from behind. She felt him push into her and, even though she could barely feel him thrusting into her, she had the pleasure of knowing that that bitch Kristen Stewart had not had him.

Belinda sighed with faux pleasure and rattled off her lines, 'Oh, baby,' 'that feels good,' and, 'yes, yes, yes.'

When Hans came, it was with the same anti-climax as the fuck itself, but Belinda told him what a great lover he was.

Thirty minutes later Hans lay snoring like a handsome water buffalo while Belinda sat on the edge of the bed, cramps surging around her middle. Bent doubled over her extended belly Belinda shuffled into the en suite bathroom. She looked in the mirror and saw a sweat drenched hag looking back at her. Using the mirror, she looked at her baby bump that jutted out in front of her like a giant boil.

Belinda jumped.

A ripple ran across the skin of her belly. She stared at herself in the mirror, holding her breath feeling waves of motion inside her. Suddenly something pressed against her from the inside, a face, twisted and grotesque appeared on her stomach as if trying to escape.

Belinda screamed.

She fainted.

The Hospital

The room was filled with flowers, roses and orchids and baskets tied to balloons saying *"Get well soon" and "Miss you"*. There were cards from fans and colleagues from all corners of the film and TV industry. A monstrous bouquet from David Tenant, a giant teddy bear from Robbie Coltrane, a basket of fruit from Brian Blessed. James Nesbitt had hand delivered two dozen roses and a box of chocolates the size of a hamper; even Kristen Stewart had sent a card with an image from *Twilight* adorning the front which went directly into the nearest bin.

The press also sent flowers together with invitations to interviews upon discharge. Some press had been invited into the hospital to see her and to take a few photos, but not the gutter press, *The Daily Mail* were kept very much out of the picture, but *The Independent*, *The Times* as well as selected celebrity magazines had been given a warm welcome. Of course nothing was mentioned about what she saw, they'd think her mad. No, she had fainted due to stress was the official story.

Belinda sat watching TV from her bed. Susanna Reid was talking to Glen Coletti about his relationship with Belinda. Belinda rolled her eyes as Glen played the victim and the role of the discarded father to Belinda's unborn child while Susanna cooed away and constantly touched his arm in desperate attempt to seem comforting.

'Have you seen this?' This from Belinda's agent, Francine, who sat in an uncomfortable chair beside her bed.

Belinda took the magazine that Francine was holding out to her. It was the latest edition of *Glamour* which had a full colour feature on Belinda including a cover shot of a pregnant Belinda in a crop top and designer slacks, hair and make-up by Krystal Dawn. Inside there was a three page story about Belinda's career and, of course, the pregnancy. The article included several photos of Belinda including one of the kiss with Tom Cruise at the premiere.

'Nice article huh?' Francine said. 'You know, Belinda, I can see the money rolling in in the bucket load. The whole fainting thing has people talking and I've had interview offers from everywhere, TV, mags, the press.'

'Can we spread the rumour that I lost the baby?' Belinda asked tossing *Glamour* to one side.

'We could, but don't you think that's a little gross?' Francine asked cautiously.

Belinda twisted her face. 'Maybe,' she said sourly.

'What about,' Francine began tapping her chin with her finger in thought. 'What about delivery? You could give a press release saying that you're going to have the baby naturally, get all mystique about it, say no aesthetic you'll meditate through the pain.'

'No, Jessica Alba already did that,' Belinda said. 'Besides, I don't want this giant thing crawling out of me, it'll split me in half, I'd have a cunt like a knocked over trifle.'

Francine laughed. 'Okay, maybe a very public C section?'

Belinda shook her head. 'Don't you think that's too Britney Spears?' she said.

A silence fell over the room, minutes passed without either of them talking. Then Belinda looked over at her agent and, measuring her words carefully, said, 'What if the rumours weren't rumours. What if I really did lose the child?'

Francine's mouth dropped open, her eyes widened in disbelief. 'You want an abortion.'

'Not exactly,' Belinda said.

'Fuck,' Francine's mouth opened wider. 'You want to induce a miscarriage?'

'Well, no,' she lied. 'I was just wondering what would happen if I did lose the thing? Asking you as an agent.'

Francine puffed out her cheeks and exhaled slowly. 'Honestly?' she said, 'I think that there would be an out pouring of sympathy, there would be talk shows, Big Brother would come knocking, they love that shit.

You could start a charity which has great tax breaks; there'd probably be a film in there somewhere.'

'So all positive then?' asked Belinda.

Francine choked out a, 'Yes,' and then, 'but you'd lose the baby.'

'Oh, of course,' Belinda said. 'I was just asking the question.'

The door opened slightly and a head appeared, young, brown skinned, a large pimple on his left cheek, bum fluff under his nose.

'Hello,' he said. 'I am Doctor Johar, could I speak to you please?'

Belinda sighed heavily and turned to Francine. 'You speak to him,' she said, 'I'm so tired.'

'Of course, dear,' Francine said, her practiced smile appearing at once. Francine stepped outside.

When she was alone Belinda closed her eyes and spoke to her baby. 'Why can't you just die,' she said, 'just fucking die and give me my life back.' She prodded the baby bump with her finger. 'Just die, please just die.'

Belinda & Francine

The doctor had told Francine that everything seemed normal. The fainting could have been due to many things including stress, a fluctuation in blood sugars or a million and one common causes that go hand in hand with pregnancy. All in all, Belinda was good to go.

Francine made a few call, mostly to the media alerting them of Belinda Ross' departure from hospital. Just under two hours later Belinda had applied her make-up, fixed her hair and squeezed into Hugo Boss sweat pants and a Hugo Boss t-shirt that was pulled up to reveal her enormous baby bump. Belinda sat in a wheelchair being pushed by Francine. As they headed towards the exit Belinda winced as a bolt of pain ran through her. She pitched forward for a second, her breath temporarily taken. Francine stopped and crouched beside Belinda.

'Are you okay, dear?' she said in a low tone. 'Do you want to go back?'

'No, no,' Belinda said through gritted teeth. 'I'm fine, honestly. Just a little cramp.'

Francine studied her friend's face twisted as it was with discomfort. 'Are you sure, dear? You don't look good.'

'Just give me a second,' Belinda said pulling herself together. 'I'm good. Let's go.'

Francine stayed crouched beside Belinda wearing a look of concern.

Belinda looked at her sternly. 'Goddamnit,' she said. 'Push me the fuck out of here.'

Francine shrugged, stood and continued pushing Belinda towards the exit.

When the doors opened the air was filled with a cacophony of shouted questions; cameras clicked and flashbulbs flashed. Members of the press crowded around Belinda held back only by a single ribbon of tape which bowed as the vultures fought for the best shot of the heavily pregnant star.

Belinda shielded her eyes with one hand and waved royally with the other. Inside she was happy, the crowd of media was more than she could have wished for and even dozens of fans had shown up to shout out their best wishes.

Belinda didn't answer any questions, feigning weakness from her *ordeal*, as it would later be called. But one question did catch her ear.

'Belinda, what was the operation for?'

As Francine followed Belinda into the back of the limousine Belinda said, 'What the fuck was that about an operation? Who told them I had an operation?'

Francine settled herself in her seat. 'Well, I certainly didn't,' she said, knocking on the partition to tell the driver to go. 'It must have been some…' Francine stopped and sat staring at Belinda, her face losing its colour.

'What?' Belinda asked.

'That,' Francine said pointing. 'Where did you get that scar?'

Belinda looked down, confused. Across her stomach was a scar approximately five inches long, it was thin and red like…it couldn't be…like something had scratched her.

Belinda and Francine sat in Belinda's comfortable apartment watching reruns of *Britain's Got Talent* and laughing at the contestants and wondering out loud if any of the judges actually had talent themselves.

Belinda had lit the apartment with candles and change into Calvin Klein PJs. The Champagne was flowing and the two friends were feeling the effects making them giggle like school girls. The conversation was casual void of work chatter, but inevitably the talk came around to the baby.

'You didn't mean it when you said about losing the baby did you?' Francine said refilling her glass.

Belinda wanted to lie but the alcohol made her more uninhibited than she would have liked and she found herself saying, 'Would that be a bad thing?'

Francine raised an eyebrow. 'Are you saying that you want to lose it?'

'I don't know,' Belinda said solemnly. 'I never really wanted children, and I still don't. This…this thing,' she said prodding her swollen middle, 'is a blessing and a curse. If I lost it then, well, you told me the benefits plus I wouldn't have a kid to look after.'

Francine snorted a laugh, Champagne dripping from a nostril.

'What?' Belinda asked.

'Nothing.'

'Say,' Belinda said.

Francine wiped her nose drunkenly on the cuff of her blouse. 'If you lost it I know a doctor who could swear you could never have children again.'

'For what reason?'

Francine winked and nudged Belinda with an elbow. 'A barren woman is a fooking gold mine.'

'Really?' Belinda said thoughtfully.

'Yep,' Francine said draining her glass. 'He's done it for several celebs.' Then, 'Oh, oh.' Francine put down her glass and clapped her hands excitedly. 'You could then adopt a Syrian baby orphan. OMG that would be so Madonna.'

Belinda laughed and raised her glass. 'A hot bath and gin it is then.'

The cramps came quickly.

The Champagne flute fell from Belinda's hand smashing against the hard wood floor.

'Jesus fucking Christ, are you okay?' Francine said suddenly sober.

Belinda put out a hand. 'I'm fine,' she forced out, before flinging her head back and screaming.

White foam began to creep from the corners of Belinda's mouth and her back arched at an unnatural angle.

Francine fumbled in her bag for her mobile phone before realising that she'd left it in the limo. 'Fuck,' she said. She scrambled to a small oak table where she knew Belinda kept her house phone.

It was gone.

'Oh shit, oh shit,' Francine panicked.

Belinda seemed to be bending backwards in half, her face contorted and grey, her mouth open wide releasing what sounded like a deep growl, primal and terrifying. Her stomach extended in front of her and seemed to be growing.

'Belinda, Belinda, can you hear me?' Francine shouted. 'What do I do?'

A small hand pushed against Belinda's belly from the inside.

Francine scuttled backwards until she hit the wall. Her knees curled up hard against her chest, her hands went over her mouth and tears ran freely down her face.

Belinda began to convulse, fresh screams escaped in coughs. Francine watched horrified as Belinda's flesh began to tear across the middle, blood running over the swollen flesh soaking into the couch.

Suddenly the flesh ripped with a wet punching sound. A small arm shot from within Belinda and began to clawing to escape. Blood spat from the torn abdomen splashing like spilt cranberry juice on the wooden floor. Belinda's eyes rolled into the back of her head and Francine heard Belinda's back break.

Francine covered her eyes, the sound of Belinda Ross, actress, client, friend being torn in half filling her ears.

Then…nothing.

Silence.

As frightening as the noises had been, the silence seemed even more frightening.

Francine opened her eyes. The body of Belinda Ross lay on the couch, eerie in the flickering candle light, foam circling her lips, a bloody hole that almost cut her in two. A pool of red crept over the floor, entrails lay in small mounds of mush on the couch and the floor and dripped from the actress' thigh with a soft wet *slap.*

Francine's jaw vibrated as she tried to swallow. She had to force her legs to move, to get out and call the police…but what to tell them. What had actually happened here?

Far in her peripheral vision she saw movement. Something was hiding in the shadows, she could feel its presence.

'Who is it?' she said. 'Please don't hurt me, I just want to leave, okay?'

Something moved quickly.

A blur really.

And then it was on her.

Something knocked her back, something small but solid. She thought it was a dog, but then she looked as it crawled from the shadows into the light. Francine's mouth moved but nothing came out, no words, no scream, all sound taken by fear, undiluted, paralysing fear. She stared silently at a face…the face of a baby. Then…it smiled…no…snarled. And attacked. It's fingers strong, it's nails like talons. Francine was helpless beneath it as it tore at her throat, ripping through the flesh, muscle and cartilage, Francine choking on her own blood. Francine didn't know how long it took her to die, but when she did it was a blessing.

The Celebration

25 Years later

As the lights in the theatre went up and the applause died, Daniel wiped a tear from his eye and tried to pull himself together. People passed him by and patted him on the shoulder as if that alone was supposed to comfort him.

His friend, Marcus, threw an arm around his shoulder. 'Let's get a drink and raise a glass,' he said.

'Lead the way,' Daniel said.

The two friends headed for the bar and ordered large JB and cokes sans coke. Marcus talked, said all the right things, they laughed and then, when it was right for him to do so, Marcus left Daniel alone with his thoughts.

He had not been alone for long when he felt someone watching him. He turned to see a beautiful blonde standing beside him, looking at him. She was wearing in a red Versace dress, her neck draped in diamonds.

'Hi, my name is Claudette, Claudette Grange, and you are?'

'Daniel Ross, please to meet you,' Daniel said with a smile.

Claudette looked surprised. 'Ross? Belinda Ross' son?'

'Yes,' Daniel laughed. 'That was my mother's tribute you just attended.'

'I was, *am*, a big fan,' she giggled. 'I read about your mother, tragic.'

'Yes it was,' agreed Daniel.

'To have your mother go into labour in her apartment, her agent delivers you and then some wacko breaks in and murders the pair of them…there's a film in there somewhere.'

'I'm working on one now,' Daniel told her. 'I've written the screenplay and producing. We're casting now. You'd be perfect to play my mother; you're not an actress are you?'

'In fact, I am,' Claudette said excitedly.

‘Then let me buy you a drink and we can talk business.’

As he turned away Claudette blinked hard. What was that she saw? She couldn’t be certain, but she could have sworn his eyes glowed red.

All In

All In

Mandarin Nights Casino, Macau
China

Part One

He was almost at the door when a large hand rested on his shoulder. He closed his eyes, composed himself and turned. The hand that had halted him belonged to a six-and-a-half-foot thug with a shaven head and tattoos, none of which said *Mother*. The thug had a face of solid granite that had forgotten how to perform any expression at all. Beside him stood a slight Chinese gentleman in an Armani suit. The man was around five ten with slick back hair and a smile that didn't give even a hint of pleasantness.

'Hello, Mr Slain, are you going somewhere?'

Daniel Slain smiled. ‘Hello, Mr Lo, sorry I can’t stop, I have an urgent appointment.’

‘I’m sure your appointment can wait,’ Lo said.

Slain gave a shrug. ‘He’ll be pissed if I’m late,’ he said.

The thug laid a heavy hand on Slain’s shoulder pinning him to the spot.

‘Not half as pissed as I’ll be if you walk out that door before we’ve had a chance to chat,’ Lo said. He looked up at the thug. ‘Longwei, Dài gěi tā zhè zhǒng fāngshì.’

The thug, Longwei, maneuvered Slain with a twist of the wrist sending bolts of pain through his shoulder. He was led through the casino with its neon lights and the *clink clink* of falling coins in the slots and the whoops of excited gamblers reaping their rewards before they inevitably lose it all again.

They passed the table on which Slain had been playing for several hours, the beautiful brunette croupier looked up as he passed by and then quickly looked away – even she knew his fate. He was steered in through a door that stood in the corner on the other side of the casino and then up two flights of stairs until they entered a plush office. The office was not as gaudy as the casino; its furnishings were deep tan leather atop a rich burgundy carpet. The walls were burgundy also, adorned with photos of Chinese temples. Cheung Lo took a seat behind a large mahogany desk while Slain was pushed into a high-backed chair facing the casino owner.

'Now,' Lo began, 'we have some business to discuss.'

Slain straightened his shirt and took a deep breath. 'I think we can come to some arrangement I'm sure.'

Lo smiled. 'Yes, Mr Slain, we can. You pay what you owe or Longwei here will break a bone at a time until you do.'

Slain fidgeted in his seat. He looked over at Longwei and quickly did a mental calculation and just as quickly decided that he could not overpower the huge oriental man. 'Look, Mr Lo, you're a reasonable man, I'm sure you can give me some time to get the money to you. What's a few dollars between friends?'

Lo leaned forward knitting his fingers in front of him. 'One, we are not friends, Mr Slain, and two, a few dollars actually equates to over five million, eight hundred and twenty thousand dollars, Hong Kong that is.'

Slain did the arithmetic in his head. 'That's over three quarter of a million US dollars? There has to be some mistake.'

Lo shook his head slowly. 'There is no mistake, Slain, my people do not make mistakes.'

'Well someone sure as hell has made one somewhere. No way do I owe that much. I could not possibly have gambled that much away.'

Lo nodded in agreement. 'This is true, Mr Slain.'

'There you go then,' he said with an air of satisfaction.

'There is the gambling obviously, but also your hotel bill, your extraordinarily large bar tab and a certain young lady and her female companion who spent a couple of hours in your room that have yet to be paid for, and you a married man.'

Slain stood abruptly. 'This is outrageous, Lo. What are you trying to say? This is fucking slander. I should sue your ass.'

Cheung Lo sat back in his chair and opened his laptop calmly and clicked a few buttons before turning it for Slain to see. On the screen was a grainy black and white photo of a slim Chinese woman no more than twenty-two sitting astride a man obviously in the throes of passion, a second young woman, white aged a little younger sat behind the first kissing her neck and cupping her large breasts.

'You seem to fuck okay, Slain, I'll give you that.'

Slain fell back into his chair and watched the onscreen action. 'That could be anybody,' he said.

The woman on the screen threw back her head. 'Oh, Slain, fuck me. Harder, harder.'

'You were saying?' Lo said with a wide grin.

Suddenly the woman seemed to stop. 'What's the matter?' she said. 'Have you come already? Is that it?'

Slain heard Longwei laugh behind him.

'Oops,' Lo said.

'I'd been drinking,' Slain said suddenly embarrassed.

'Well, she is a beautiful girl,' Lo said turning the screen back to him and turning it off. 'I'd come quickly too…maybe not as quickly as that but…'

Slain ran his hands over his face. His heart raced, his temples throbbed and sweat had broken out on the back of his neck. He looked up at Cheung Lo sitting behind his desk looking smug. He felt so stupid. He couldn't be like a normal gambler and get into money troubles that would lose you your house or send you to GA meetings for the rest of your life, no, he had to get in deep shit with fucking Cheung Lo, the man who could kill you so badly that your children's children would feel it, if he had had any children that is. He knew that he could not pay, and he knew that he could not talk his way out of it, but how much did Lo want the money? Maybe there was bargaining to be done after all.

'Mr Lo. Truth be told I don't have the money. We have options here. You can let me go and I will get the money for you via some payment scheme maybe or you can kill me right here, right now. If you kill me then you won't get a penny of what's owed obviously. The choice is yours.'

Lo rubbed his chin and pretended to be thoughtful. Eventually one of his emotionless smiles touched the corners of his mouth again. 'I think I can think of a third option, Mr Slain,' Lo said.

'Anything,' Slain said. 'I want to do what is right.'

Lo smiled broadly but Slain didn't like the way it looked on his face. 'Follow me, Mr Slain,' Lo said pushing back his chair and moving around his desk. 'A man of excess should like this.'

Slain hesitated but Longwei once again took his shoulder in a vice like grip and steered him after Mr Lo. They went down the stairs that had taken them to the office and back out onto the floor. Slain thought of screaming for help, but who in their right mind would want to confront a man of Lo's influence and power. He couldn't even signal for help as those who did look in his direction, of which there were very few, immediately turned their eyes to the carpet upon seeing who was leading the way.

They walked through the casino, passed the cashier's desk and numerous poker tables, passed the slot machines and the sequinned covered waitresses with trays of alcohol. Then, all of a sudden, Lo disappeared through a doorway. Slain was maneuvered through the doorway also, down a narrow badly lit corridor and in through another doorway. They entered a plain room with magnolia walls and a tiled floor. Beneath a single strip light stood a wooden chair in front of a TV.

'Sit,' Mr Lo said pointing to the chair.

'What is this?' Slain said getting worried now.

'Just sit,' Lo said calmly and waited.

Slain hesitated again, but no physical encouragement from Longwei this time. The two Chinese men just waited patiently until, out of ideas, Slain sat facing the TV.

Mr Lo began to pace the room, his hands clasped behind his back, his back bolt upright, his head high and proud. 'Mr Slain,' he said eventually. 'By your own admission you do not have my million dollars.'

'Three quarters of a million,' Slain corrected.

'With interest that's one million.'

Slain opened his mouth to speak, a blow to the back of the head with a spade sized hand quietened him.

'I have two unhappy girls who can't afford their college fees until they've been paid by you,' Lo said. 'I have a casino that looks like a fucking charity because of you. I mean, I'm a business man, Mr Slain, and business men need to be paid. So you can't pay, so what are we to do? I'll tell you, I'm going to invest in you, Slain. You see, before you made money disappear I was watching you and you were winning. In fact, you were winning so much that I ear marked you as a potential risk in my casino. I watched you play and you were good, damn fucking great, Mr Slain. So, I'm going to give you the chance to win back my money.'

Slain looked confused. 'Win it back?' He frowned deeply at Cheung Lo. 'How can I win the money back? I have no money to play with.'

'I'll stake you,' said Lo grinning.

Slain eyed Lo with suspicion. 'I owe you a million bucks and you are gonna stake me more money to win it back?'

'Exactly,' Lo said.

'And what if I lose?' Slain asked.

Lo looked excited now. He rubbed his small hands together and picked up the remote to the TV. 'What is important to you, Slain?'

'Sorry?' he said

'Important. What is important to you?'

'You've lost me, Lo,' he said.

Lo clicked the remote and the screen turned white and then focussed. A black and white picture showed a grimy looking room filled with boxes, it looked like a warehouse somewhere. The camera moved, lost focus again and when the picture sharpened he saw the face of a young man. The man had short black hair, a handsome looking face but scared eyes that darted this way and that.

'Glen,' Slain whispered.

'Yes,' Lo said. 'This is Glen your best friend in the entire world. Glen saved your life once when you were children, you nearly drowned, but Glen dove in after you to save the day, but of course you know this.'

'What the fuck are you playing at, Lo?' Slain barked.

'Now now, Mr Slain,' Lo said with a chuckle. 'Glen is quite safe with my people, quite safe that is as long as you win. If you lose well…you'll be one best friend short.'

The screen went white again but when the picture returned the face of Glen had been replaced with that of a blonde woman in her early thirties. She was beautiful, but she too looked scared.

'Contestant number two,' Lo announced. 'Fail me twice and your dear friend Joanne breaths her last breath.'

'You fucking bastard,' Slain shouted and launched himself from his chair towards Lo. Lo stood his ground, but before Slain reached him Longwei delivered a bone crunching blow to Slain's stomach. Slain doubled in pain and hit the ground. As he tried to suck in oxygen he looked up at the screen to see it change once more.

'Hello, Jessica,' Lo said as Slain's wife appeared on the screen. 'How can you fuck around on this woman?' Lo questioned. 'Look at her for fuck sake. That raven hair, those eyes, those cheek bones. Jesus, Slain, if I had a woman like that I'd be banging her every night, forget teenage whores.'

'Don't you fucking touch her,' Slain gasped still stunned from the blow. 'I'll fucking kill you.'

Lo crouched down beside Slain and looked at him. 'Lose three times, my friend, and not only will I have your wife killed I'll let my men take turns fucking her in every hole she has, and even a few I'll have put in her.' He stood and turned to Longwei. 'Get him cleaned up and sitting at the special table. I want him playing poker within the hour.

Part Two

The Game

The table was set in yet another back room. The edges of the room were bathed in shadow and in those shadows Slain could just make out the figures of men passing their weight from foot to foot, solid looking figures waiting for someone to make a wrong move or say the wrong thing. The table in the centre of the room was brightly lit, the shocking green so familiar to him over the years he could smell it. On one side of the table was a skinny looking man wearing the croupier's uniform of black trousers, a white shirt with the sleeves rolled up and a burgundy waistcoat and bow tie. The man was stone faced, his hair shorter at the sides than on top and light stubble. His hands moved at speed as he shuffled the cards and cast them one by one to the other side of the table.

In receipt of the cards sat four men. He knew two of them, George Harrison, no, not that one, this George Harrison was in his late fifties with white hair and hard sapphire eyes that never gave anything away; his calloused hands gathered up his cards which he barely looked at before waving away another card.

To his right was the other man Slain knew, Francis Jacoby. Francis was in his mid-thirties and had developed lots of facial tics, a twitch of an eye here, a twitch of a lip there. He had developed them over the years to hide any indications of the hand he was holding as you never knew which twitch was his cards or which was his natural state.

The third chair was taken by an older serious looking gentleman with cropped greying hair and large round glasses that made him look like an owl.

Next to him was an empty chair and next to that was a nervous looking man in his thirties, Slain guessed. His suit was shabby with dark patches under the arms, his hair was plastered to his head with sweat and he held his cards in trembling hands. Slain guessed that the man must be in the same position as he was right now.

Slain nodded to the two men he knew as he was led to the empty seat and sat down. Slain watched as George Harrison received his winnings for his hand. The dealer dealt Slain in on the next hand. Slain was about to tell the dealer that he had no money when one of the shadow goons shouldered him aside and placed a pile of chips in front of him. Slain gave them a glance and reckoned that there was at least two million American dollars.

Pictures of his two best friends and his wife flashed through Slain's mind like a speeded up slide show.

Slain picked up his cards – Jack of diamonds, three of clubs, ten and six of hearts and a seven of spades. Slain pushed the buy in bid in front of him and tossed his cards in the centre of the table. 'Fold,' he said. He watched the rest of the table place their bets and ask for new cards. He stared at his pile of chips, weighing up his options, trying to put together some kind of plan that would get him out of this mess.

Slain heard a groan around the table and looked up to see Francis Jacoby having chips pushed towards him. A new hand was dealt and again Slain looked at his cards – a pair of twos, a three, a nine and a king.

‘Fold,’ Slain said and tossed his cards back to the dealer. He didn’t even know what he was doing but he thought it may buy him some time to think.

On the table the bets began to rise with George Harrison and Francis Jacoby taking the lead. The Owl Man shook his head and folded when the bets got into five figures. The Sweating Man shook nervously as he pushed chips in front of him until he had no more to bet with.

Francis’ eye fluttered and his tip lip jerked three times. ‘Raise one hundred thousand,’ he said.

Harrison pushed forward two hundred thousand. ‘Raise one hundred grand.’

Francis offered him a twitchy grin. ‘Raise another two hundred thousand.’ He pushed the required chips seven inches from his cards as per poker protocol.

‘I have no more chips,’ the Sweating Man said.

‘Are you out then, sir?’ asked the croupier.

‘My hand, I want to bet on my hand.’

‘But you have no more, sir.’

‘Please,’ he said looking at Slain, ‘please lend me some money.’

Slain looked at the Sweating Man's pathetic expression, pleading in his eyes, his bottom lip quivering like a child.

Slain shook his head sorrowfully. 'I'm sorry, I can't.'

The man ran his hand over his face and looked down at Slain's pile of chips. 'I'll pay you back after this hand, I promise I'm good for it.'

'I can't,' Slain said again. 'Sorry.'

'I'll stake you,' Harrison said to the man.

'Harrison, don't,' Slain said. 'Leave him.'

'The man wants money, Slain,' Harrison said. 'He reckons he can beat me, let him prove it, I've got plenty.' Harrison looked passed Slain to the Sweating Man. 'How much you want, kid?'

The man grinned like a mad man. 'Loan me half a million.'

Slain turned urgently to the man on his left. 'Are you fucking crazy?' he snapped. 'Do you have any idea who these fucking guys are? Don't do it, man.'

'Shut up,' the man spat. 'I need this.' He looked over to Harrison. 'Deal?' he said.

Harrison pushed one million towards the croupier. 'The kid's bet and I see him.'

'Fold,' Francis said. 'Too rich for my blood this time.'

'Okay, kid,' Harrison said. 'Show me that winning hand.'

Breathing heavy the Sweating Man placed down his cards. 'Four aces.' The man beamed as he saw Harrison hesitate. His hands readied to pull the pile of chip towards him.

Harrison sighed and placed his cards on the table. 'Straight flush, kid.'

The room seemed to freeze for a second. The sweating man stared at Harrison's cards, five, six, seven, eight and nine of clubs.

The silence was broken by the Owl Man whispering, 'Fuck.'

The Sweating Man began to shake uncontrollably. 'I need more time,' he said to the room. 'I just need more time, please. Help me,' he said looking at Slain.

'I'm sor…'

A man stepped from the shadows behind the Sweating Man and threw a solid arm around his neck jerking his head back. The Sweating Man struggled, kicking out and clawing at the arm that held him tight. The shadows man raised his free hand in which he held a slim bladed knife. Before Slain had time to move out of the way the man brought the knife down plunging it into the Sweating Man's eye. The Sweating Man went into spasm as the shadows man held him tighter. The knife was pulled from the eye socket and pushed into his throat just below the chin. Blood splashed on the table and across Slain's shirt.

A few seconds later and the Sweating Man was dead. The shadows man dragged the body into the darkness behind the chairs and he was gone. Slain looked at the other men and the croupier, only the Owl Man showed any emotion and even he was trying to swallow it down.

'While we reset the room there will be a short break,' a disembodied voice said from outside the room.

The players got up and moved out of the door. When Slain exited Longwei was waiting for him. He opened the door to the room with the TV and motioned for Slain to enter. Slain went into the room where Mr Lo was waiting. He asked Slain to sit. When he was seated, Mr Lo spoke.

'What is all this folding shit, Slain?'

'My hands were shit,' he said.

'But you didn't even ask for more cards, just folded…twice.'

'I…I know what I'm doing,' Slain said lying.

'Well, let me make sure you do know what you're doing.'

The TV screen lit up. His friend Glen sat tied to a chair, behind him was a unidentifiable figure dressed all in black.

'What the fuck are you doing?' Slain said, his heart rate suddenly rising.

'Watch,' Lo said. 'You need to win back my money, Slain,' Lo continued. 'I told you what would happen if you lost, and folding is losing.'

The man in black stepped up to the back of the chair to which Glen was tied. Glen twisted his head this way and that trying to see behind him. 'What are you doing?' Glen said. 'Why am I here?'

The man in black grabbed Glen roughly by his hair. Glen yelled out and began to struggle against his bonds.

'Don't do this,' Slain said looking at Lo.

Lo smiled and nodded at the screen. 'Ssh, you're going to miss the best bit.

The man in black pulled out a knife with his free hand and held it up so that the camera caught it's glint. He then took the blade and pushed it into Glen's temple. Glen screamed in pain, blood flowing down his face in thick black ribbons. As the tip of the knife met the bone of Glen's skull the man in black slammed the butt of the knife with the heel of his hand forcing the knife deep into Glen's temple. He then jerked the knife out, blood sprayed from the wound. The man in black threw Glen's head forward and stepped back.

Slain watched his friend sit there dead. He tried to rise but sat back down as Longwei approached. 'You piece of shit,' Slain told Lo. 'I'll fucking kill you for this.'

Lo raised an eyebrow. 'Now you know I mean what I say perhaps you'll play cards.' He motioned towards the door. 'Shall we see if they are ready?'

Slain walked from the room, his legs felt weak and the image of his dead friend made breathing difficult. He entered the poker room and took his seat alongside Owl Man. The croupier waited until all were seated and then dealt the cards.

Over the next hour Slain played every hand, some he won, some he lost and was coming out even. Then he picked up his cards and he had to stop himself from showing any joy at all. In his hand were three tens, a six and a nine. Slain held his breath and tossed the six at the dealer. The dealer, in return, gave him a new card. Slowly he turned it…a nine. Slain slowly and deliberately placed his nine next to the other.

'Raise one hundred thousand,' said Owl Man.

For the first time Harrison wore an expression, that of a smirk. He pushed a tower of chips forward in front of him. 'I see that and raise four hundred thousand.'

Owl Man swallowed hard and looked at the croupier as if he had the answers. 'Fold,' he said eventually and placed his cards in front of him timidly.

'I will see that and raise a million dollars,' Slain said dropping his chips onto the table.

'I'll call that,' Francis said.

Harrison squinted at Slain unsure of himself at last. 'I'll see that bet, Slain,' he said.

'What do you have there, boy?'

Slain smiled and laid down his cards. 'Full house, tens over nines.'

Francis flipped his cards. 'Threes over sevens,' he said.

Harrison casually turned his cards one by one, Slain watched an iron fist gripping his heart with every card. 'Full house too,' Harrison said. 'Kings over queens.'

As the chips were pushed towards Harrison. Slain began to panic. 'I need to take a break,' Slain said and got up from his seat.

As he exited the room Mr Lo was waiting. 'You can't do this, Lo, please.'

'Let's go,' Lo said.

Slain was led into the room and sat forcibly in front of the TV. Slain knew what was coming. He felt ice cold as the TV screen showed his friend Joanne sitting tied to a chair. Behind her stood a man in black as there had been behind Glen.

'Don't do this,' Slain pleaded. 'I'll do anything, just don't kill Joanne.'

Lo smiled and nodded towards the TV. Slain bowed his head but Longwei hooked a large hand under his jaw and forced up his head.

The man in black stepped forward and caressed the face of Joanne with gloved hands. Joanne squirmed under his touch and tried to turn her head away. 'Don't fucking touch me,' she said. 'Keep your hands off me.'

'Feisty,' Lo said.

The man in black reached further down and began to grope his victim's breasts. Joanne rocked in her chair. 'Get your fucking hands off me you piece of shit. Get the fuck away from me.'

The man in black released her and took a step back. Nothing happened for a second and Joanne seemed to calm. Then, in a blur of movement, the man in black raised something in the air and the next thing Slain saw was his friend's head split in two. The man in black pulled the axe free from her skull and Slain watched as blood sprayed in all directions, brain matter spilled down the front of his friend's chest. Slain jerked and vomited at his own feet.

Lo *tutted.* 'Mr Slain,' Lo said handing him a handkerchief. 'Clean up and get back in there, your wife is counting on you.'

Part Three

Conclusions

Slain retook his seat at the table. His heart felt heavy in his chest and his head felt as if someone were drilling into it. He watched the cards land in front of him, he scooped them up and looked at them but he could not even see what they were. The next few hands were a blur, he won only one hand and that was in a daydream state so he didn't even know what he was doing, just betting blindly. In the end Slain resorted to folding, once not even looking at his cards. At this a man stepped from the shadows behind him and placed a photo of his wife, Jessica, in front of Slain. Slain stared at it, tears running down his cheeks. He looked along the row of three men but each had their heads down looking at their cards, no one gave a shit what was happening to him, but why should they? Did he give a shit when the Sweating Man was in trouble? Did he lift a finger to help him? No. So why should anyone help Slain now.

'Mr Slain,' the croupier was saying. 'The bet is three hundred thousand.'

Slain had not even looked at his cards. As he did so he realised that he had not had a chance to change a single card lost as he had been in his own depressive state. He looked now and placed them face down in front of him. 'I call and raise five hundred thousand,' he said.

'Are you sure, Mr Slain?' the croupier said.

'Yes,' Slain said.

'Gentlemen?' the croupier said to the table.

'I'm out,' Owl Man said throwing in his cards.

'I'll call that bet,' Francis said.

'I'll call that bet and raise three hundred thousand,' Harrison said raising an eyebrow as if to dare anyone to call his bet.

Francis examined his cards thoughtfully tapping his finger against the table. 'I think…I'm out,' he said setting down his cards.

'Just me and you, Slain,' Harrison said.

'How much do you think I have in front of me?' Slain said, 'about nine hundred thousand? I'll call and raise six hundred thousand.'

There was an audible gasp from Owl Man and Francis shook his head in pity for Slain.

Harrison pushed his chips towards the croupier. 'Call and raise five million.'

Slain didn't flinch, he was too numb to feel any emotion. 'Lo, if you're listening I need cash,' Slain said in monotone. 'Lo, give me cash. I want five million now.'

'Jesus, Slain, are you fucking insane?' Francis said.

Slain fired him a look. 'Shut the fuck up, Jacoby,' he said. 'You play your cards and I'll play mine, oh yeah you folded, well, boo-fucking-hoo.' Slain looked up in the air as if talking to a deity. 'Lo? Give me five million, give me five-fucking-million.'

There was silence in the room for what seemed liked forever and then the door opened and Longwei entered carrying a small suitcase and placed it in front of Slain. Slain opened the case and did some mental arithmetic. 'There's five million here,' Slain said. 'All in.'

Harrison closed his eyes and sighed. 'You really want to do this, Slain?' Harrison said looking over at him. 'You sure you want to do this?'

'Shut the fuck up and play poker,' Slain said dead pan. 'Unless you want to fold, play.'

'Oh I'll play,' Harrison said.

The croupier nodded at Harrison. 'Sir?' he said.

All eyes fell on Harrison's cards as he laid them face up for all to see. Eight, nine, ten, Jack , queen of hearts. 'Straight flush, my friend, sorry.'

Owl Man threw back his head, 'Fuck,' he said.

Francis Jacoby shook his head sadly.

Slain looked down at Harrison's cards and his eyes stayed locked on them for a few long seconds. Then he placed his cards in front of him; ace, king, queen, jack and ten of spades. 'Royal flush,' Slain said.

'Yes,' Owl Man said punching the air as if he had won.

'Well, I'll be damned,' Francis said.

For once Harrison smiled, a great beaming smiled that spread right across his face. 'You son-of-a-bitch,' he said to Slain. 'Well played, my friend, well played.'

Even the croupier smiled, not a beaming smile but enough to convey his pleasure.

Slain was expressionless. He had won more money than he knew what to do with but he had lost his two best friends this evening.

Minutes later Slain had gathered all his chips and filled the suitcase and a large canvass bag that the croupier had had beneath the table. He made a quick phone call and then carried his winnings out of the room.

Lo was waiting alongside Longwei.

Slain handed him the suitcase. 'There's three million in there along with a million interest,' Slain said. 'The croupier has the five million loan. I believe this is mine,' he held up the canvas bag.

'I guess you earned it,' Lo said smiling without humour.

'I'll never step foot in this place again,' Slain stated. 'You'll never see me again. But before I go I have one last gift for you.' He handed Lo a phone, 'Enjoy.'

As Slain left the room Lo looked at the phone, there was a paused video on the screen. He pressed play and watched, confused. The camera moved through a darkened house, down a hallway, up the stairs and through a door. Lo strained his eyes to see what was happening. There was a whisper.

'Lights.'

Someone turned on a torch and shone it onto a bed where a young oriental woman was sleeping. A man stepped forward and punched the woman in the stomach. The woman shot awake, her face turned screaming towards the camera.

'Liling,' Lo said in a panic seeing his wife on the screen.

The man wrapped Liling's hair around his hand and dragged her from the bed screaming. Lo watched his wife kick and yell, calling out to him in the chance that he may appear suddenly to save the day, but Lo could not save anyone. He watched helplessly as the man withdrew a serrated bladed knife and, holding Liling firmly by the hair, started to cut. The man drew the knife from one temple around, under her chin to the other temple. Liling was hysterical now, her screams piercing Lo's heart. The man dropped the knife and, forcing his fingers into the cut under Liling's chin yanked upwards peeling the woman's face from her skull.

Lo dropped the phone not wanting to see his beautiful wife taken apart. 'Longwei. Kill that mother fucker. Take his fucking eyes from his head, kill that piece of shit.'

Longwei spoke to his boss quietly. 'There is one more thing,' he said.

Lo looked up at him, his eyes filled with tears. 'What?'

Longwei raised a gun and pointed it at Lo's head. He pulled the trigger, the wall behind Lo instantly painted with bloody modern art.

Longwei's phone rang. He answered it on the third ring.

'Is it done?' Slain's voice asked.

'It is,' Longwei said. 'Thanks for the cash.'

'My pleasure,' said Slain. 'My pleasure.'

Fuck Dr. Seuss

(a non- moral tale)

Fuck Dr. Seuss

(a non-moral tale)

T'was the night before Christmas and Noel looked out from the upstairs window as families gathered outside of his shop, their coats speckled white with snow and their faces wearing grins that were reserved for this time of year. The little kiddiewinks laughed and spoke excitedly in squeaky tones that went right through Noel's bones. The annoying little bastards would soon be within touching distance and it was this thought that made him wish he had a cattle prod at hand. Why did people have to change just because it was Christmas? Wasn't there enough fakery in the world as it was? Even in WWI the Germans and the allies stopped their obsession with killing each other to have a game of football…Jesus, how sick was that.

Noel hated Christmas, he always had. He loathed the false smiles, the pressure to enjoy the day, the emphasis on family. Noel hated Christmas cards, Christmas trees, decorations, Santa and especially

Christmas songs. He hated that Christmas began in September - fucking September for Christ sake. And then when the day finally came he was forced to sit around a table with people he didn't even like, wear a stupid paper hat and watch a stupid Christmas movie – *White Christmas, It's A Wonderful Life, Miracle on 34th Street, The Grinch* – The Grinch? Fuck Dr. Seuss.

Noel felt sick watching the excitement on the poor moronic faces. He knew that it was all an illusion. He had never been fooled, never taken in, not even as a child, even though he had been born on the very day he hated. Yes, Noel had been born on December 25th. Many people had been jealous of this but he didn't know why, it wasn't like he had gotten tons more presents or anything, in fact, his tight-fisted parents had used it as an excuse to buy him one lot of presents and say that they were Christmas/birthday gifts. He had been told that his Action Man had been a Christmas/birthday present – how could that be? If his birthday had have been in June would it be the same? Would he have gotten the torso for his birthday and have to wait until Christmas to get the legs? Playing for half the year with a soldier who was the victim of a vicious IED incident? He didn't think so. And when he received the gift of the Wings album, *London Town*, would he have gotten the songs *London Town*, *I'm Crying* and *Girlfriend* at Christmas but have to wait until his birthday to hear *Morse Moose and The Grey Goose* and *With A Little Luck*? He didn't think so. Mind you, he hadn't wanted the album in part or its entirety as he hated Paul *smug bastard* McCartney as much as he hated Christmas.

Another thing he had hated about Christmas as a child was being dragged from one relatives home to another, here they all sang *Happy Birthday* and gave him the same "joint" presents and told him he had been born on the Lord's birthday – what a load of bollocks. His final stop on the relative's tour was at his granny's house. This final stop had been the worst memory of his childhood. Okay his granny was kind and fed him cake until he was sick, but the nightmare that haunted him was that of the wrinkly old face zooming up on him and her soft, fat, moustachioed lips covering his face in kisses; the very last kiss being planted firmly on his own lips like the attack of some incestuous Facehugger from the *Alien* movie. Even to this day when the clock struck midnight and the dreaded day was upon him, his brain automatically and involuntarily conjured up that nightmarish memory that sent him cold with fear.

But even without the wet grandma snog and the whole gift debacle, Noel would have still hated Christmas. He just could not enjoy a time of year that had a stupid twat from *X Factor* at number one in the charts, that showed the same stupid, unrealistic, supposedly heart-warming movies on TV, that had people going off to church that had never been in their lives before, that had people eating until they burst with no other reason than *it's Christmas*; crass, sickening over sentimentality…

'Excuse me, Noel, where do you want me to put the delivery of candy canes?'

Noel looked down at the staff member. She was half his age, about twenty-one, very attractive with long auburn hair and deep green eyes. She was wearing an elf's costume that he had given to her as a uniform. He had made sure that the costume was a little too small so that it emphasised her large breasts and her tight little ass.

‘Put them in the back room next to the mince pies,’ he told her.

He watched the girl walk away and thought that he may have to promote her to head elf if she did some work on *his* candy cane later.

Noel’s Toy Emporium was a unique toy shop, unique in the fact that it only opened one day a year – Christmas Eve. This, to other business men, may have been a fool hardy thing for him to do, but, in fact, Noel had turned into a very rich man. You see, every year all the toy shops would run out of the countries favourite toys before December 24th; parents would stress and children would howl as if their world had fallen apart because they could not have the toy that their friends were sure to have. Noel had taken advantage of this very fact and surmised that, if he stocked his shop with every toy and only opened on Christmas Eve then there would be a mass rush and he could earn enough money to last him the rest of the year. He even thought that if the parents wanted the toy badly enough then they would pay for it and so he increased his prices by 100%. The plan had worked and he had made more money than he ever imagined. Every Christmas Eve there were long snaking queues around the block waiting for the doors to open. People would camp outside for days with lists as long as the queue, hoping to get that special present to stop their child from moping around the house for the next twelve months.

Noel would get a buzz from the frazzled expressions as the doors opened. He loved the panic that turned into aggression as parents reached for the same toy at the same time. *Black Sunday* had nothing on Christmas Eve at Noel's Toy Emporium. It was a gladiatorial battle that resulted in bloodshed. He had watched from the balcony outside of his office high above the action; he had installed CCTV for the purpose of capturing the mayhem then would re-watch it later editing the highlights to make a *Best Of* DVD.

Those were the good ole days that made Christmas Eve worth the wait. But something had happened these last couple of years, something that had taken back the fun. You see, the whole idea of the store was to create and observe panic, the last-minute scramble for that perfect gift; but now, that beautiful aggressive melee had become the odd tame skirmish, isolated incidents that were nothing more than a snatch and harsh words. It wasn't even worth filming.

People knew by now that Noel's Toy Emporium was the place to buy the last-minute gift and so their visit to his store had just been factored in to people's Christmas routine. If one could not find the gift that they were looking for then, on Christmas Eve, they would flock to Noel's toyshop with the comforting thought that he will stock what they needed – COMFORTING??? Noel did not deal in comfort!! But there it was, instead of making people crazy he was making them… HAPPY. The very thought of someone being happy at Christmas because of something he had done made him nauseous. He was not The Grinch, he was not Ebenezer Scrooge, he would not be redeemed…EVER!!

He had to do something to stop the awful pseudo seasonal joviality that he hated so much. He could not bear the thought of people coming into his store wearing those pathetic Christmas smiles and, dare he think it, wishing him a 'Merry Christmas'. He wanted to punch every one of them in the face just for thinking it. Something had to be done, misery had to be brought back to Christmas. And then he thought of it. An ingenious idea. An idea that was beautiful in its conception and would bring him unbelievable pleasure – to him at least.

Christmas Eve had been busy like every other. Noel's little helpers – all young women in their uniforms that were too small – had been busy stocking the shelves with every toy or game or delicious treat. The overstuffed bastard he had hired to play Santa was ensconced in Santa's Grotto, and he himself would open the doors for the first time ever. The advertising had been hitting the local papers, TV and radio stations for months.

"Noel's Toy Emporium will be holding a special Christmas Eve opening, selling all the latest toys PLUS toys you will not be able to find ANYWHERE else. This will be Noel's last hurrah as the store will be closing its doors forever after this Christmas Eve."

And so it was. A goodbye gift to himself, and what a goodbye he hoped it would be.

'Excuse me, Noel,' it was the scrumptious little elf again.

'Yes, errrr, what?'

'It's Emma, Noel,' she said.

'Ah, yes, Emma,' as if he gave a shit. 'What is it that you want?'

'Just wanted to say that it's a couple of minutes off 9am, you wanted to open the shop.'

'Thank you,' he said, 'I'll be right down.'

'It's so exciting, isn't it?' she said beaming. 'I absolutely adore Christmas.'

'Do you,' he said rhetorically. 'I'll be sure to give you a gift that equals your enthusiasm.'

The stupid girl jumped up and down and clapped her hands. 'Thank you, Noel, that's so sweet, I can't wait. May I kiss you?'

'Later perhaps,' he said, 'after we open.'

'Okay, I won't forget,' she teased. Then she skipped away leaving Noel to think of the Action Man and the IED and he wished he could blow Emma's legs off just to stop her fucking skipping and bouncing.

At 9am Noel unlocked the doors hearing the crowd get excited outside. On the last lock he pretended that it was stuck just to leave them outside in the cold a couple of extra minutes. When eventually the doors opened the crowd of people poured in. There were thousands of men and women and children of all ages. The advertising had been ultra-successful; people had come from all over to see the *new* toys that could be bought nowhere else. Noel instructed the parents that it was okay for their children to run about his shop on their own, he had set up meeting points around the store so that they may re-join their family after they had shopped. The parents were delighted, it was one more worry off their mind. The children too were delighted to be free of the watchful eye and scornful tongue of their parents.

For a couple of hours, the now usual scene played out, Noel had to hold down his breakfast as he saw people smiling and laughing as his store brought happiness and joy. But that was okay, the fun had not yet started.

A scream rang out from the rear of the store. Everyone stopped, scanning the store for their children hoping they were safe, but it was just an over enthusiastic mother who had found the toy of her son's dreams.

Colin and Megan Hogworth were shopping for their teenage daughters. They were a family that adored Christmas and Christmas shopping. They both had stressful jobs, Colin was a traffic warden and Megan worked for Arriva Trains, so they both spent the year being hated…Christmas was their "fun time". Their daughters, Helen and Helena, were also huge fans of the season and loved to decorate the house inside and out, covering the house in twinkling lights and giant plastic reindeer in the garden. They were a family that were proud to receive a special award by the local council for most decorated house in the street. Megan loved to cook Christmas dinner where the four of them would sit down to a 28lb turkey with all the trimmings.

Helen and Helena would sit every Christmas Day and cry while watching *Noel's Christmas Presents* as some old wrinkly was reconnected with some other old wrinkly from their past. The girls watched as the oldies cried for the camera while looking disappointed at who they had found, and wishing they hadn't bothered at all. In the afternoon they would visit their grandparents dressed in their new Christmas clothes and give them gifts of aftershave, slippers and a new bed pan for Grandma Hettie.

Colin and Megan had come to the store this Christmas Eve to find something specific – a family onesie set. They had all gotten super excited at the newspaper ad about Noel's Toy Emporium's big day. In a photo that had accompanied the article had been a set of onsies that looked like reindeers, they even had hoods with antlers on them.

Colin and Megan had been in the queue outside for nine hours. They had arrived at midnight with folding stools, muffs and flasks of coffee, prepared to face the weather that, according to reports, was going to be bitter with heavy snow and plummeting temperatures.

They found themselves a couple of dozen people back and spent their time cheering themselves along by singing Christmas carols and telling everyone about their “wonderful daughters”. It was a mini holiday for them full of adventure.

At 6am Colin and Megan began to get excited in anticipation of the shop opening. They stopped singing *We Wish You A Merry Christmas* for the umpteenth time, jumped up from their folding chairs and began to sing, “Why are we waiting.” At 8am the singing stopped and was replaced with a mantra of, *“Nearly there,”* and *“I see movement inside.”* At 8.30am the countdown began, first every minute and then, in the last five minutes, every second was counted out loud. When the shop opened Colin and Megan went crazy, screaming and shouting and hooting.

As they entered the shop they immediately made their way to the clothing section, here they found costumes and Christmas jumpers and – onesies. In an attempt to hold on to the excitement a little longer they decided to buy each other a Christmas jumper before looking at onesies.

‘What are you going to have, my Snuggle Blanket?’ asked Colin.

‘I don’t know, Bunny Nose,’ giggled Megan, ‘there’s such a selection. How about this?’

Colin looked over as Megan held up a jumper in front of her that looked like a Christmas pudding.

‘Ahhh, you look good enough to eat,’ he told her.

‘Oh you old charmer,’ she cooed. ‘Now you, now you.’

Colin held up a jumper in front of himself. ‘How about this?’ It was a snow scene with a 3D snowman, an orange nose stuck straight out for about five inches from his chest.

‘Oh, you look adorable, Snoochie Chops.’

‘I’m going to get this,’ Colin said excitedly. ‘I’ll wear it on Christmas day.’

‘Oh no you won’t,’ Megan said.

‘Oh yes,’ Colin said with realisation.

‘ONESIES!!!’ they screamed in unison.

They quickly moved to the onesie section and scanned the racks; there were teddy bear onesies and tiger onesies, Superman and Batman onesies, Scooby Doo and Stormtroper onesies and then there were reindeer onesies.

Colin and Megan squeaked with excitement. They searched through the rack for their size, but the label said **one size fits all**. Colin held up one of the onesies and frowned, 'I'll never fit in this,' he said.

'And there's something in the material,' Megan said.

Colin gave it a feel. 'It's probably stitching, Monkey Cheeks, these things are usually made in Taiwan and the craftsmanship is quite under par.'

'Actually,' said a voice.

They turned to see Noel, the shop owner, standing behind them wearing a beaming smile.

'These onesies are a favourite of mine,' he said. 'One size fits all is a perfect description. They may not look big enough, but they are designed to expand or contract to fit any body shape. And what you can feel in the material, madam,' he said to Megan, 'is wire.'

'Wire?' she said.

'Yes,' Noel said. 'The wire is there to protect the shape without interfering with the softness and comfort of the garment, this way the onesie will look just as good in five years' time as it does now.'

‘Let’s take them,’ Megan said excitedly.

Noel saw that Colin looked a little unsure. ‘If they don’t fit,’ he said, ‘if they are not the most comfortable onesie you’ve ever worn, then I’ll refund you every penny, guaranteed. Once you put them on, you won’t be able to take them off.’

Colin looked at his wife’s wide smile and the pleading look in her eyes. ‘Okay, we’ll take four,’ he said.

Rosemary Pepper-Jones had been standing in line outside of the toy store since 10pm Christmas Eve Eve. Her companion had fallen asleep almost immediately leaving her to stay awake and guard their place in the queue. Rosemary had brought her six-year-old daughter, Emily, along with her, as Emily had said, *‘I don’t trust mummy to get the right thing.’* The Christmas before there had been three days of tantrums because the doll house Rosemary had bought Emily had not had an en suite bathroom in the main bedroom. Rosemary was determined that this Christmas she would save herself the grief and bring

Emily to choose her gift, a doll that she had seen in an advertisement in one of the papers. Emily had demanded the doll immediately, it cried and burped and spoke like a real human baby, apparently, it even pooped, but Emily would not be dealing with that, that's what a nanny was for.

Rosemary had awakened Emily a minute before 9am and when the doors opened Emily pulled her mother into the store screaming, 'This way mummy. Hurry up, come on.'

Rosemary followed her daughter through the store until she spotted the doll section. Emily stood in front of shelves packed with dolls of all shapes, sizes and colours, there were brunette dolls and blonde dolls, red headed dolls and dolls with cornrows; there were dolls with dummies, dolls in summer dresses, in designer jeans, in ski clothes; dolls dressed as nurses or school teachers, black dolls, Asian dolls and white dolls.

But Emily started to stamp her feet and cry.

'Whatever is the matter, Emily?' her mother asked.

'They haven't got it, mummy,' she balled. 'We were too late, *You* were too late.'

‘Calm down, dear, mummy will find a member of staff, perhaps they have some in the store room.’

Emily threw herself to the floor and began to wail and thrash about.

Rosemary looked embarrassed. ‘Emily, get up, do you know what germs are down there.’

‘Can I be of assistance?’

Rosemary turned to see the tall, handsome gentleman that had opened the door this morning. He glanced at her daughter writhing on the floor and then back to Rosemary.

‘We were wondering,’ Rosemary said, ‘if you had anymore dolls.’

‘Was there a particular one you were looking for?’ Noel asked.

‘The one from the paper that talks and cries and such.’

Emily jumped to her feet and ran to Noel, she stood staring up at him, hands on hips. ‘Are you the shop assistant?’ she asked.

‘I am the owner of this shop, young lady,’ Noel said, staring down at her, wanting to slap her little face.

‘I want the doll from *The Times*, the one that’s like a real baby.’

Noel exaggerated a thoughtful expression. ‘Let’s see, do we still have one left?’

‘I WANT ONE, I NEED ONE, now, now, now,’ Emily screamed precociously.

Noel looked at Rosemary and pulled on a smile. ‘I think I have some in the store, if it’s okay I will take your cherub to see?’

Rosemary looked concerned. ‘Without me?’

Noel laughed. ‘She’ll be fine, Miss. I’ll take good care of her.’ He leaned in close, ‘You look like you could do with a break and the café does a great Irish coffee.’

Rosemary blushed. ‘If you’re sure,’ she said, ‘that would be nice.’

‘That’s settled then,’ Noel said. ‘Little Miss, you’re with me.’

Emily squealed and grabbed Noel’s hand. ‘Let’s go.’

Noel mouthed, ‘She’ll be fine,’ and walked away with Emily. Once out of her mother’s sight Noel squeezed Emily’s hand.

‘Ow, that hurt, Mister.’

Noel said nothing.

‘Fuck, I can’t wait ‘til Christmas, I’m gonna get so fucking gurped.’

‘You can always tell when you’ve had a good Christmas, you can’t remember it yo.’

Mike and Clarissa had been in the queue since 8am but the way it snaked down the street and around the corner didn’t worry them. They were twenty years old and they were in love with Christmas. For them it was the perfect excuse to get drunk out of their tiny minds.

Clarissa was tall and slim with a tiny waist and breasts like firm pillows. Her hair was long and dark and perfectly framed a fresh, tan face of youth, with a smiled that never waned and eyes that still held hope. Mike had burning looks and a physique that he had had to work at to stave off the physical repercussions of drinking. He wore a shirt that was too small and jeans that were low hung, showing off half his underwear even in December.

Mike and Clarissa had fallen in love in a bar close to their university. He had seen her through an alcoholic haze and slurred something inappropriate that she was too drunk to see as such. She had giggled and they had fallen into a corner and groped around for a while. The next day they had woken up in Mike's bed, clothes strewn around a dirty flat, slashes of sick on the bathroom floor, dried ejaculate on Clarissa's cheeks, and decided that this was love.

Now it was their first Christmas together and they needed gifts. They should have bought them by now but with the drinking, smoking pot and more drinking, they hadn't found time.

'We at a party tonight,' said Clarissa. 'We have to be quick here cause me wants to do some pre-party drinking. Are we dressing up?'

'Of course, woman,' Mike said. 'You gonna wear that red number? You look the bomb, girl.'

Clarissa smiled and pulled Mike close kissing him passionately. 'I'm gonna make your bomb explode,' she teased.

‘We need to hurry and get in there,’ Mike said. ‘I want some pre-party pussy. And remind me I gotta get me some ting for my rents innit.’

‘Ya brah, gotta get my sis’ some bling,’ Clarissa said.

‘It’s a toy shop,’ Mike whispered, ‘ain’t no bling but tinsel.’ Mike patted his pockets. ‘Have you got the dough?’

‘Nah, brah, you carrying,’ Clarissa said looking shocked.

‘Nope, cupboards are bare, woman.’

‘Dumb fuck,’ she snapped. ‘This is crump. We’re gonna have to jack some ting and get outta there.’

Mike didn’t want to steal, last thing he needed was to be hog tied by some pig and miss the party. ‘Okay, let’s jook,’ he said eventually.

When the line began to move it moved quickly and they were soon at the door, Clarissa brimming over with excitement. As they entered a suited man bumped head on into Clarissa.

‘Watch it, granddad,’ she snapped.

Mike said nothing, he had considered the man’s eyes and not liked what he saw.

Noel looked the young couple up and down. 'You looking for anything in particular?' he asked.

'What's it to you?' Clarissa said.

'Shut up, Clarissa,' Mike said, still nervous of the stranger.

'Well, if you're looking for some ting rad and a bargain, there's a little room just to the right of Santa's Grotto, some cool tings in dar, choice shit. Go looksie, but don't tell anyone.' Noel tapped his nose. 'Our secret, brah.'

As Mike and Clarissa walked away Mike said, 'What do you think, cuz?'

'I think he talks funny,' Clarissa said, 'but let's check it out.'

Stan O'Brien was in his fifties and had little in his life but for his wife, Doris, and his son, Jack. He had worked as a labourer for twenty odd years until he met Clarence who told him that he could earn more money being unemployed that employed if he knew the loop holes. Stan had done his research and now lived a comfortable life compliments of the state, all he had to do was tell a few white lies, like registering as disabled, and *kerching!* There were other ways of conning for profit too outside of the benefit system, last year he had been on national TV telling a breakfast programme how all the presents for his family had been stolen in the night and that they had nothing for Christmas but tears. Donations had flooded in. By Christmas day the house was filled with all kinds of gifts. Of course, there had been no burglary, but no one was to know that, it was just a little white nationally advertised lie – and it worked.

Stan had another ace up his sleeve. He had seen on TV people that had queued to be the first into stores on promotions day, and the first one through the door was always pulled aside and given a huge cheque or some tremendous award for their dedication. Stan's plan was to be that first customer and had thus queued with his son for twenty-six hours. He bounced on the balls of his feet waiting for the doors to open.

Jack was twelve, but looked much older because of his obesity. The dumpling of a boy had never enjoyed Christmas all that much, except for the food of course. His gifts were always jumpers that never fit properly or socks that squeezed his chubby feet. But he hoped that this year would be different. He had seen an advertisement in his father's *Nuts Magazine* of a skipping machine. The machine turned the rope without the use of friends to do it, which was perfect, because Jack didn't have any friends. He had pestered his mother and father every day until they relented, and they could only buy it from Noel's Toy Emporium.

As Stan and Jack entered, Noel greeted them with his practiced smile. 'Hello, sirs, welcome to the store.'

Stan waited as people rushed passed him to find their gifts.

Noel kept the smile, though he could feel it wavering.

'And?' said Stan.

'And, enjoy your shopping?' said Noel.

'And, where's the cheque?'

'Sorry, sir, you've lost me.'

'The cheque,' repeated Stan. 'I was the first in the queue, people who line up all night get a cheque…or a huge gift.'

Noel considered. 'Really?'

'Yes,' Stan said getting irritated. 'It's fact.'

'Fact, is it?' Noel said. 'In that case, I have the perfect gift for your son. Why don't I take him to where it sits and you shop for whatever you like?'

Stan eyed Noel with suspicion. Would the gift be good enough for his son? Would it be expensive enough? 'Ok,' he said eventually. 'But if it's not a good enough gift for my patience in line I'll be complaining.'

Noel looked down at Jack. 'This way, little boy.'

The room was small but all the seats had been taken and others stood around the peripherals of the room. At the front of the room was a small stage and microphone. When all the doors had been locked Noel took to the stage.

'Ladies and gentleman,' he began, 'welcome. Now, who loves the song *Do They Know It's Christmas*?'

There went up a collective cheer, men, women and children *whooped* and clapped.

'Well, I am here today to talk about this classic.'

Another cheer.

'Sung by Bono, George Michael and a collection of other millionaires, this song resonates with us all. Let us examine the lyrics – *'There won't be snow in Africa this Christmas time…'*

There were, *'Awwwwws,'* from the crowd.

'Well, yes there is fucking snow,' Noel said, followed by the crowds audible gasps. 'There is snow in the Drakensberg Mountains and Mount Kilimanjaro. There is even ski resorts in Morocco. Just emotion blackmail.'

'What is this?' someone shouted.

'You fucking moron,' someone else called.

'No rains or rivers flow,' Noel continued. 'There are fifty-two rivers in South Africa alone; The Nile, the longest river in the fucking world runs through eleven African countries. This song is written by fucking idiots, and you morons are fooled by this shit.'

People began to descend on Noel, tossing their chairs to one side and making their way to the stage. Noel backed away smiling. He slipped out through a rear door and locked it, trapping the people inside. He pushed a button to the left of the door as he heard people inside banging to get out and kill him for sacrilege. The button released gas that would fill the room in five minutes, in six they would all be dead.

'Merry Christmas,' Noel laughed. Then he heard something that chilled his bones – someone was playing *Merry Christmas Everybody* by *Slade*.

Jack O'Brien had been lead into a room in which there was a special gift. Noel had left him there, Jack, wearing a smile across his fat face like a dent in large pink pumpkin. The room was decorated in thousands of fairy lights and tinsel and Jack stared around the room as if someone had dropped him off in Heaven. In the centre of the room was a wrapped gift, but not some twelve inch super hero doll of a gift, this present was huge, standing six feet tall and twice as wide, Jack moved towards it with caution. There was a card attached that read, *For Jack, Merry Christmas*.

Jack began to excitedly open the present, ripping the paper with enthusiasm. When he finally finished Jack could have cried. It was the skipping machine he had wanted. Two tall silver men stood facing each other with a metal rope between them. Jack had visions of him being slim, having friends and being able to eat cake without putting on too much weight.

There was a large red button on the men's belts, Jack pushed it. There was a whirring sound. Both the robotic men began to swing their arms and as a result the rope began to turn.

Jack got very excited. 'I love Christmas,' he said clapping his thick hands. 'I L-O-V-E Christmas.'

As the rope rose Jack stepped between the two men and as the rope descended he jumped in the air and the rope passed beneath his feet. Jack jumped and jumped, the smile widening with every leap. Suddenly as the rope swept over his head and moved down his left side it tightened and quickly swept from left to right slicing through Jack's legs cutting neatly through flesh and bone. Jack's rotund body fell to the floor next to but separated from his short fat legs. His dying body thrashed about in an ever-growing pool of his own blood.

Noel watched through a small window in the door. He grinned as he watched the child die, the loud choking sounds sealed off from the world by thick soundproof walls.

'Merry Christmas, fatty,' Noel whispered.

Noel made his way through the store and up the staircase that led to his lofty office from whence the music was coming. Noel had given strict instructions that his office was out of bounds to everyone; it was his sanctuary to which he would go to sit and escape the morons that came into his store. He liked to sit and listen to his music, bands such as *Tidelands*, *Don't Believe in Ghosts* and *Sirens in The Delta*, okay, not world famous bands, but he loved them; the commercial shit, the David Guettas and Mark Ronsons of this world, pissed him off. As for Slade? He couldn't stand that Noddy bastard at the best of times let alone Christmas. Every time he heard, *'It's Chriiiiiiiiimas!!'* he wanted to shoot Noddy in the fucking face and spit on the corpse.

He took the steps to his office two at a time and flung open the door. There he saw a dancing elf, the girl who he had fantasised about fucking on many occasions. She turned and saw him, a smile leaping to her lips.

'Don't you just love this song?' she said, then, 'wait,' she paused waiting for her moment. 'It's Chriiiiiiiiismas!!'

Noel stepped forward and picked up a CD that the stupid girl had readied to play, *X Factor's Christmas Number Ones*. This infuriated him further and he seized the girl by the hair, yanked back her head and snatched the CD across her throat opening it up like a second smile. The girl's hands went to her throat immediately, streams of red running from between her fingers.

As she dropped to her knees, her eyes wide with shock, Noels leaned in close. 'I fucking hate that song,' he said.

Emma the elf fell face down on the floor of the booth. Noel stepped gingerly around the snaking stream of blood and hit eject on the CD player. He threw the Slade CD next to the body of the dead elf and slipped in a disc by *The Electric Hearts* and left the booth.

Mike and Clarissa stepped into the room suggested to them by the suited stranger. The room looked like someone's living room decorated in red tinsel, a Christmas tree in the corner and an open fire in one wall, it wasn't a real fire of course, it was paper flames blown by a fan and lit by an orange light, but the room was warm as if it were real. Pinned to the mantelpiece above the imitation fire were two large stockings, both stuffed to capacity with presents; beneath the Christmas tree were more presents all wrapped in colourful paper and tied with bows.

'Wicked, yo,' Mike said.

'Dis is da bomb, brah.'

The two started with the presents beneath the tree. Unwrapping them they found a watch for him and her, perfume by some second-rate celebrity, a calendar of over made up twentysomethings from some "reality" show, slippers that looked like Santa (hilarious), chocolates shaped like penis' and a Michael McIntyre DVD box set.

The kids grabbed a sack that lay nearby and filled it with the presents, all but the Michael McIntyre DVDs, not even they were that stupid.

‘We can get cheddar for this shit, yo,’ Mike said. ‘Let’s split, girl.’

‘The stockings, brah,’ Clarissa said.

‘Nah, girl, too sus, yo. We got enough wiv dis.’

‘Don’t be a pussy,’ she said. ‘Be bamf, BF.’

Mike rubbed his chin, unsure.

Clarissa stood with her hands on her hips making sure that Mike could see how fine she was. ‘Yo want any ba dink-a-dink tonight, brah, you better help me gank those stockings.’

Mike licked his lips. ‘Dang, girl, y’all C-4. Let’s do dis.’

They both unhooked the stockings and were about to leave.

‘Wait, let’s see what swag we got, yo,’ Clarissa said. Before Mike could protest she pushed her hand into the stocking and rummaged around. Mike watched as his girlfriend’s eyes turned from a look of curiosity to the look of shock. When she screamed, Mike jumped out of his skin. Clarissa pulled her hand out of the stocking, well, her wrist anyway, her hand was now missing and blood pumped from the chewed-up stump. Clarissa's screams became hysterical and Mike panicked.

'Fuck dis,' he said.

He hung the stocking back on its hook and as he did so it pressed a lever which released a panel from either side of the fireplace. A long bladed sword shot from behind each panel and skewered Mike and Clarissa, entering their gut and exiting backs. Streams of blood ran the length of the blades and dripped heavily on the hearth rug.

For a moment, they both stood and gawped at the weapon that pinned them, then Mike reached out for his girlfriend in a final attempt to touch her one last time, but they both slumped and died before his hand could reach her.

Noel was watching from behind a two-way mirror in the wall. He chuckled to himself. 'Merry Christmas, yo,' he said.

Emily Pepper-Jones was shown into a black room and the door locked behind her. Emily was confused at first, the room was bare, with no sign of a doll anywhere. Then music began to play and the walls began to turn, lights of every colour shone, bathing the room in a rainbow; the turning walls revealed shelves, shelves filled with dolls, thousands of dolls. Emily, for once in her short life, was speechless. This was the most amazing thing she had ever seen, she stood in awe and watched the walls finish turning. All the dolls were identical except for what they wore, some wore riding breeches, some wore ball gowns, some wore a wedding dress, but all were blonde with hard blue eyes that shone in the light.

Emily walked down the rows of dolls inspecting them like she was a sergeant major in the army. She would stop every now and then and finger the hem of a skirt or stroke a dolls face. She was fascinated by how realistic they were. She wanted to see how they worked, how it talked, how it peed, could she make a doll cry? She stopped in front of a doll dressed in lederhosen and picked it up. Emily squeezed the doll, but nothing happened, so she squeezed the belly hard with both hands. She felt something hit her toes. Emily looked down to see brown sludge sliding off her black patent shoe. She looked confused and turned the doll upside down to see that the sludge had actually come from the dolls anus. Emily immediately dropped the doll with a look of horror and hopped around the room trying to wipe the doll poop off her shoe.

'Uuggggghhhhh, that's disgusting,' she said.

She jumped around some more until she had cleaned all remnants of dolly shit off her Gianvito Rossi pumps. Then she examined the dolls again and found one that looked like Mrs Santa Claus; Emily snatched it up and held it at arm's length and squeezed its belly – a single tear rolled from its eye. Emily was excited, she had found the doll she was looking for, a doll she could make cry.

'Cry baby,' Emily said to the doll, 'cry for Christmas.'

Emily deliberately and violently squeezed the doll, jamming her fingers into the dolls stomach. Suddenly the tear ducts opened and a thick spray of acid ejected from the doll directly into Emily's face. Emily dropped the doll and threw her hands over her face, feeling like her skin was on fire, the pretty child turning instantly into a monster of disfigurement. She tried to scream but the acid had also sprayed into her mouth burning her vocal cords, rendering her dumb.

Blindly, the child stumbled around the room, her mind filled with her mother's face. She needed her mummy now. The pain was excruciating. She needed it to stop. Emily reached out a hand to feel where she was going and it fell upon a door handle; she twisted it and pushed, falling into a snow storm. The snow was coming down thick and heavy, the drift up to her knees. Emily's hands were still on her acid caked face as if holding the peeling flesh could make the pain go away – it didn't. She wandered for a while like a wounded animal and then something happened that came as a relief – she fainted.

The agonising pain had gotten too much and the child's body had reacted in the only way it knew how, by complete and utter shut down. Emily fell face down in the snow.

Noel stood and watched the whole scene unfold. 'Now every time you look in the mirror,' he said out loud, 'you will remember Christmas Eve. Merry Christmas, little girl.'

Children lined up with their parents outside of Santa's Grotto waiting to see Father Christmas. Of course, every normal person knows that Santa is like God – he doesn't really exist – but to these little children he was magical. Santa was, in fact, Barry Munger, who Noel hated on the same par as Noddy Holder. Barry did have some good traits, he was honest to the point of being offensive, he didn't give a shit what people thought of him and he'd once punched Louis Walsh in a theme park. But the one thing that Noel despised him for was his undying love for Christmas.

Barry would become a different man at Christmas. Instead of his usual morose demeanour he would laugh and smile and actually be pleasant, he would even stop shouting expletives at his neighbour, at least 'til Boxing Day. It was annoying. Why would someone so foul become different because of a date on a calendar? So, Noel had hired him to play Santa, and hired him for a very special reason.

Barry was dressed the part, a bright red Santa suit, thick black boots and a beard specially designed by Noel himself. Because Barry was so goddamn fat he needed no extra padding under his tunic and he wobbled that fat gut every chance he got, laughing out an irritating, 'Ho, ho, ho.' Barry was in his element. The grotto was filled with fairy lights and fake snow and two female elf helpers in tiny outfits all tits and legs. 'Merry Christmas to me,' Barry thought.

The children came in one by one and sat on his knee and asked for gifts that they were sure not to get. Steven wanted a fire truck with eighteen different sounds, Mary wanted a make-up set by Beyoncé and perfume by Sarah Jessica Parker, Kevin wanted a Barbie doll dressed as an air stewardess, Gayle wanted a Leona Lewis CD that Santa would never give her as he could not abuse a child's ears like that.

The next little boy in line stepped forward confidently full of baby bravado.

'What's your name?' Santa/Barry said, as the boy climbed up on his knee.

'Marvin,' he answered loudly.

'Have you been a good boy, Marvin?'

'Yes,' he lied.

'That's good,' Santa/Barry said. 'What would you like for Christmas?'

‘More Christmas,’ he said, bouncing up and down, ‘I love Christmas.’

‘So do I,’ Santa/Barry said. ‘It’s a wonderful time of year for happy hearts and families.’

‘I love you, Santa,’ Marvin said and hugged his hero.

‘Ho, ho ,ho,’ Santa/Barry said hugging the child.

Marvin sank into Santa’s chest and let out a satisfied sigh. Then out of sheer devilment he gave Santa’s beard a tug. When the beard was tugged the special design of Noel’s came into play, and the earpieces released two ultra-sharp razors, when this happened the downward momentum of the beard caused the razors to slice through Santa’s ears and cut them from his head. Blood poured from Beneath Santa’s hat and an ear dropped onto the child’s lap.

Marvin screamed at the top of his lungs with fear and Barry joined him, but from unbelievable pain. The screaming duet were soon joined in their chorus by the pretty elves when they saw what was happening, and as the parents rushed in they too joined the cacophony of fearful cries.

Noel made his way through the store observing the crowds of Christmas zombies with their plastic smiles hiding their stress, he despised every single one of them smug in their cotton wool fantasy that Christmas made everything okay. He raced passed the chaos at Santa's Grotto and made his way to a room at the far end of the store. He let himself in by tapping in the entrance code that only he knew. Once inside he did two things. One was to push a button that automatically locked every door in the store except for the exit door that led from the room he was now in. Secondly, he opened a large chest which was filled with plastic Jesus'. He picked one up and twisted the crown of thorns which set the timer for the bomb that was hidden inside of the cross and tossed it on top of the other C-4 stuffed Jesus'. Noel dashed to his car and sped away in time to watch in the rear-view mirror as the Jesus chest exploded setting off a chain reaction of explosions from explosives placed throughout the store. The windows blew out, flames ripped through his store and, if he listened closely, he could have sworn he could hear the screams of the Christmas lovers being burned to death.

'Merry Christmas, one and all,' he said, as he drove away.

Christmas Day

Before the sun had risen, the household was filled with Christmas spirit. The Hogworths were wearing smiles specially reserved for those overly affected by lunacy. They flitted around each other constantly saying, *'Merry Christmas,'* and tensing with excitement.

The morning began with the Hogworth family tradition; the two daughters, Helen and Helena, made Hogworth Christmas pancakes topped with fruit and a gallon of maple syrup. Helen and Helena constantly and involuntarily looked at the presents beneath the tree, the anticipation building like a bubbling volcano ready to erupt.

After the pancakes, as if to delay the present opening still further, the Hogworths would wash the dishes and only then would they gather together around the tree sitting in the same order as they did every year, Colin, Megan, eldest daughter, Helen, and the youngest, Helena. One by one they would open a present each, first reading the attached card and then tearing it open like someone possessed, sometimes with an accompanying squeal.

As the present giving ended and all four were in gift Heaven, Colin coughed to get everyone's attention.

'As you know,' he said to the girls, 'me and your mother went shopping on Christmas Eve and we bought a special present for all four of us.' Colin brought forward four parcels and passed them out.

They all took a deep breath and tore off the wrapping paper. The two girls howled with delight when they saw the reindeer onesies. They instantly threw off their dressing gowns and slipped into the onesies, Colin and Megan grinned at each other and did the same.

'The shop owner said that once we put them on we won't be able to take them off,' Colin said.

'It's so soft and warm,' Helen said.

'Let's zip them up together,' Helena said. 'One…two…three.'

They all zipped up the onesies at exactly the same time and pulled up the hoods revealing a big red nose and antlers. The girls jumped up and down and howled some more.

Beep!

The nose on each of the onesies lit up.

'It pinches a little,' Megan said.

Helena squirmed. 'It hurts.'

'Dad,' Helen said, 'what's wrong?'

Colin tried to unzip his onesie but the zipper wouldn't move.

'What's wrong? Colin, what's going on?' Megan said, panic in her voice.

Each of them pulled and pulled at the zippers.

'It's getting tighter,' Colin said, anxiously pulling at the zip. 'I can't...get...the fucker off.'

The mechanics of the onesies were intricate and Noel had been designing the suits for twelve months or more. When the zipper was zipped fully it locked the onesie so that the wearer could not remove it and the wires in the onesie began to constrict, it was a great feat of engineering.

‘Mummy, daddy, help,’ Helena squealed, her face turning purple.

Blood began to soak through the onesies, the whole Hogworth family were shouting now, not even able to move to try and free themselves from the reindeer onesies.

The outfits grew tighter and tighter, crushing all four, skin split and bones began to break, blood pooled at their feet.

Helen was the first to die, the hood squeezing her skull until it fractured and broke apart crushing her brain. Megan died next, but only seconds before Helena whose cheekbones shattered, her eyes popping from her head, her teeth jutting from her mouth as her whole face collapsed.

Colin lay dying on the floor literally half the man he had been. The sound of his large bones breaking was deafening. His blood ran from his onesie and slithered across the floor, soaking into a card that had come with the onesies; it read –

Merry Xmas, Love Noel xx

Contact

www.jjamesauthor.wixsite.com/rainbow

www.facebook.com/jjamesbooks

twitter: @JJames_author

Instagram: johnjames_author